DREAMS OF TOMORROW

When artist Jessica Lawrence was jilted, just before her wedding, she determined to concentrate on her career and ignore men. However, at a party she meets contented bachelor Ian Grantly. There is a mutual attraction which they both fight against. Then, during holidays in Cornwall and Italy, the attraction grows. But whilst Jessica believes that he will never settle down, and Ian thinks that she may return to her fiancé, how can they ever find happiness together?

Books by Toni Anders
in the Linford Romance Library:

A LETTER TO MY LOVE
DANCE IN MY HEART
RIVALS IN LOVE
NEVER LET ME GO
A NEW BEGINNING
THE SWEETEST FEELING
LUCREZIA'S SECRET
THE HOUSE ON THE SHORE

TONI ANDERS

DREAMS OF TOMORROW

Complete and Unabridged

LINFORD
Leicester

First published in Great Britain in 2011

First Linford Edition
published 2012

British Library CIP Data

Anders, Toni.
    Dreams of tomorrow. - -
    (Linford romance library)
    1. Love stories.
    2. Large type books.
    I. Title II. Series
    823.9′2–dc23

    ISBN 978–1–4448–1286–2

Published by
F. A. Thorpe (Publishing)
Anstey, Leicestershire

Set by Words & Graphics Ltd.
Anstey, Leicestershire
Printed and bound in Great Britain by
T. J. International Ltd., Padstow, Cornwall

This book is printed on acid-free paper

First Steps

'Is this seat reserved or may I join you?' Jessica looked up from contemplation of the depths of her coffee cup. What she saw was far more interesting. She almost forgot she wanted to be alone.

Six feet of lean, tanned, dark-blond masculinity topped off with a crinkly smile was enough to challenge the resolution of the Ice Queen herself. But Jessica was made of sterner stuff. She eyed him with complete indifference.

'I believe there are thirteen stairs in the average house. I only require one so that leaves plenty for you.'

'I don't want to sit behind you. We'd look like we were playing buses. Couldn't we sit on the same stair?'

'Why?'

He ushered her into the room next door where they found a corner and a small couch. Ian perched on the arm

1

and began to attack his plateful.

'Hello, you two. Enjoying yourselves?'
A short, blonde girl had appeared in
front of them, smiling happily. 'I didn't
know you knew each other,' she went
on, without waiting for an answer. 'Ian,
mind you behave yourself. Jessica's not
like your usual girls.'

'Don't attack me when I have a plate
of food in my hands,' he chided. 'And don't
give Jessica the wrong idea about me.'

The smile Hilly gave him showed
what she truly felt about him.

'Is he really your cousin?' asked
Jessica. 'Or is that another piece of his
nonsense?'

'He really is my cousin,' said Hilly.
'Aren't I lucky? He can be absolutely
charming when he likes, but some-
times . . . '

'That's enough,' Ian broke in. 'Don't
warn her off. I had enough trouble
getting her here.'

He bent forward, kissed Hilly on the
cheek and handed her his empty plate.
'Off you go and see to your guests like a

good little hostess.'

'See you later.' Hilly twiddled her fingers at them.

★ ★ ★

Jessica finished her supper, and Ian took her empty plate and put it on a table nearby. Then he seated himself next to her.

'More comfortable than the stairs,' he said. 'Or would you prefer to go back there? I only want your comfort.'

Jess looked at him. 'Why did Hilly tell you to behave yourself?'

'She's a bossy boots. Always was. When I was a child, I felt as if I had two mothers.'

'But Hilly must be younger than you.'

'What difference does that make? You can be a bossy boots at any age.' He picked up a cushion, punched it a few times and put it behind his head. 'This is so relaxing,' he said with a sigh. 'A comfortable seat, soft music and a beautiful companion.'

She looked at him. 'Actually, I'm not your companion,' she pointed out. 'I just happen to be sitting here.'

'But at my invitation. So technically you *are* my companion.'

'Must you always have the last word?'

He sighed again. 'Must you always be argumentative? It's a party. Enjoy yourself. Or can't you? Did you come under duress?'

Jessica considered. Hardly duress, but she had been persuaded. Her first thought had been to decline the invitation. She wasn't in the mood for parties. But Hilly had kept on and on: she must get out, meet people. There were other apples on the tree, and so on.

'I was persuaded,' she admitted at last. 'I didn't want to come but Hilly talked me round.'

Before he could ask any more, a man came into the room and looked around hurriedly as if seeking someone. Spotting Ian, he came over.

'There you are, Ian. You're wanted on the phone.'

Ian jumped up. 'Thanks.' He turned to Jessica. 'I've been expecting a call. I gave them this number. Excuse me. I'll be back. Don't go off with anyone else.' And he disappeared through the nearest doorway.

Immediately Jessica stood up and went in search of Hilly. She found her in the kitchen refilling plates with nibbles.

'It's amazing how popular these are. This is the second time I've refilled them. Do you want a coffee?'

'I'd love one,' Jessica said. 'What about you?'

'Thanks. That's a beautiful outfit.' Hilly cast an admiring glance at her friend's hyacinth blue dress. 'No wonder Ian fell for you. Where is he, by the way?'

'Gone to take a phone call.' Jessica pushed a cup of coffee towards Hilly.

'Thanks. I'll just take these into the dining-room than we can have a chat.'

She was soon back.

'So, glad you came after all?'

'It's a lovely party. I'm just not in the party mood yet. But thank you for inviting me.' Jessica smoothed the skirt of her dress. 'It gave me a chance to wear this. I bought it for — ' she gave a shuddering sigh ' — for my honeymoon.'

As Hilly came round the table and gave her a hug, Jessica stiffened.

'No, don't be kind, I shall cry. In fact, I think I'll go now — '

'Right, I shan't be kind,' said Hilly. 'I'll be cruel. You are not going now, you're going back into that room and you're going to dance and enjoy yourself.'

'But — '

'But nothing.' Hilly glanced towards the door. 'And here's your partner. Hi, Ian! Jessica's going off to dance. Why don't you both go? I'm going to wash a few glasses, we're getting short.'

Ian gave Jessica a flourishing bow. 'May I have the pleasure?' Firmly possessing himself of her hand, he led her into the room where the music was beginning again and a few couples were slowly circling.

She went into his arms and had to

admit that their bodies fitted together perfectly. He placed an arm firmly round her waist and his lips on top of her head, and took a deep breath.

'Please don't sing,' she said quickly.

'Sing? Who said I was going to sing?'

'You took a deep breath. People do that when they're going to sing.'

He leaned back and looked down at her. 'Remind me to practise shallow breathing when I'm with you.' His arm tightened round her and they swirled into a corner and out again. 'As a matter of fact, it wasn't a deep breath, it was a sigh. A sigh of pleasure.'

Jessica said nothing.

'Don't you want to know why I gave a sigh of pleasure?'

'I suppose you like dancing.' She didn't sound very interested.

'Doesn't dancing give you any pleasure?'

'I love dancing.'

'So why — ?'

'I'm just not in a party mood.' She stopped and dropped her arms. 'Wouldn't

7

you like to find another partner? I'll square it with Hilly if you're afraid of her.'

He stared at her for a few minutes in silence, then, putting an arm about her waist, he walked her to the door.

'Come on, we'll collect a drink and go outside for a bit. The garden is lovely and the fresh air might help.'

She tried to pull herself free but his grip was firm.

The kitchen was empty. Ian poured white wine into two glasses, passed one to her and, taking the other, led her out into the garden.

'There. That's better, isn't it?'

Jessica had to agree that the terrace, perfumed by a bed of night-scented stock, was preferable to the warmth of the room inside. Cool air fanned her cheeks. The quietness soothed her.

Music and laughter receded into the distance. They found a seat at the end of the terrace and sat down, sipping their drinks. Ian said nothing, waiting for her to speak first.

She gazed into the darkness of the garden, lit only by tiny lights threaded amongst the branches.

'I'm sorry.' Her voice was so quiet he had to strain to catch her words. 'I'm spoiling your evening. But it's your own fault. You should have left me on the stairs.'

He slipped an arm along the back of the bench behind her head.

'I'm a man who loves a challenge. You're my challenge for this evening.'

She blinked and in the light of the lantern above their heads he saw the glint of tears on her lashes. His hand left the bench and curled round her shoulders. Gently he drew her towards him.

'No.' She pulled away. 'I'm finished with men. I don't want affection from any man, thank you very much.' She stood up. 'I'm going back inside.'

He caught her hand and held her back. 'I'm sorry. Please sit down. Let's talk. No affection, I promise. Just talk.'

She looked down at him. 'All right. Just for a little while.' She sat down again.

'How long have you known Hilly?' he asked.

'We were at school together — I told you that, didn't I? It wasn't a close friendship, but we knew each other. When we left, she went to secretarial college and I went to art school, so it was years before we met again. We bumped into each other a few weeks ago and hit it off.'

'So you're an artist. What do you paint?'

'Houses, mostly. People commission me to paint their homes. That's what I'm doing here. Hilly wants a painting of this house as a present for her mother.'

'Her mother, Ramona Penn, the famous novelist,' Ian said solemnly.

'Don't you like her? She's your aunt, isn't she?'

'She is. I haven't seen her for years. She spends most of her time in Italy. As a small boy, I was terrified of her. I probably would be even now. Aunt Ramona is a very forceful character. She forced poor Hilly to become her secretary, regardless of what Hilly wanted to do.'

'I think Hilly has an interesting life,' Jessica said. 'She divides her time between this beautiful house and a villa on the Italian lakes. Anyone would envy her.'

'Would you like to live in Italy?' Ian asked with genuine interest.

Jessica considered. 'Who wouldn't? It would be wonderful to visit.'

'So why don't you go and live there for a while? Plenty of lovely buildings to paint. Is there anything — or anyone — to keep you in England?'

She turned away and he heard a tremulous sigh.

'I'm sorry,' he said hastily, 'I didn't mean to pry.'

'It's all right. It's finished now.'

He waited for her to continue, and when she didn't, he asked gently, 'What's finished?'

'My engagement. The thing that would have kept me here.'

He looked at her. Her hair shone in the moonlight. He thought she was very lovely. What a pity he wasn't looking for a relationship himself.

'Do you want to talk about it?'

'No. I've gone over and over it in my mind. I want to forget it — and him.' She shivered and he was all concern.

'Come on. Let's go back inside and find something to warm you up.'

She allowed herself to be guided towards the garden door. He wanted to put his arm round her but was afraid it might annoy her. He risked a hand on her waist as they reached the door and stepped inside.

'Smelled the coffee pot?' Hilly asked, pouring out three mugs and pushing a jug of cream towards them. 'Did you dance?'

'For a while. We've been sitting outside,' Ian told her.

'Bit cold for that. Here.' She draped a warm, soft shawl round Jessica's shoulders. 'Can't have you catching cold before you've finished my commission.'

'What time may I come in the morning?' Jessica asked.

'Not too early,' Hilly said with a grimace. 'I'll need a little lie-in after all this. Come about eleven.'

Jessica nodded. 'I need to take some more photographs first, so if you're not around, I'll make a start on them.'

'Can I come and watch?' asked Ian.

'Certainly not. I need to concentrate.'

'And you couldn't concentrate with me there?'

Jessica didn't deign to answer. She finished her coffee and replaced the mug on the kitchen table.

Ian stood up and took her hand. 'Come on. Let's try another dance. Exercise will warm you up.'

She allowed herself to be led into the room where a dozen or so couples were moving slowly to a soft, smoochy tune.

'Nice and gentle,' Ian murmured, taking her in his arms. 'And no singing.'

*   *   *

Gradually Jessica began to relax. The movement was soporific. She felt as if she could fall asleep drifting to the music. Why was she worrying about Gregory?

Why was she even thinking about him? She was in the arms of an attractive man who really seemed to like her, who certainly wanted to be with her.

Catching Hilly's eye across the room, Ian smiled. Hilly returned the smile, then cast her eyes upwards. Ian's charm had worked again.

Later, when the party began to break up, it took the combined efforts of Jessica and Hilly to persuade Ian to leave.

'I'm staying for a while to help Hilly tidy up,' Jessica told him.

'I can do that too. Many hands make light work, and so on.'

'You've never tidied up anything in your life,' said Hilly sternly. 'Your mother does all that.'

'I know, and it's not fair,' said Ian. 'I never get a chance. I might be very good at tidying up if someone would let me try.'

'Go home,' said his cousin.

'I want to see Jessica home safely,' he argued.

'I'm staying just down the road,' said Jessica. 'I'll be quite all right.'

Ian sighed. 'Seems I'm outnumbered. Will you give me your phone number so that I can call you tomorrow?'

When Jessica showed no sign of doing so, he sat down in the nearest chair. 'I shan't go until you do,' he said, eyeing her defiantly.

'Oh, all right.' Jessica scribbled her number in a small notebook, tore out the page and handed it to him. 'Now goodnight.'

Ian looked at them sternly. 'You're not to talk about me when I'm gone.'

'Talk about you?' said Hilly scornfully. 'D'you think we have nothing better to talk about?'

While Jessica began to load the dishwasher, Hilly carried another tray of dishes over to the draining board. Ian stood hesitantly in the middle of the room.

'Right, then. I'll go.'

The girls made no reply but dealt busily with the dirty dishes.

'Mrs Dexter will be in in the morning to give the place a good clean before I leave for Italy,' said Hilly, 'but I don't want to leave all these dishes for her to deal with.' She turned to Ian. 'Are you still here?'

'Going. Going,' he said, holding up his hands defensively. 'See you soon, Hilly. I've really enjoyed myself. Goodbye, Jessica. I'll call you.'

The girls watched him go and as soon as the front door slammed behind him, they burst into subdued laughter.

'Poor Ian,' said Hilly, 'he did so want to stay. He's afraid we'll talk about him, that I'll tell you all his faults.'

'Has he any? I got the impression he was perfect.'

'He has been brought up by a doting mother to *believe* that he's perfect,' said Hilly, 'but he doesn't really think it. It's just his flippant way of talking. Actually he's one of the nicest men I know.'

'He was very kind to me tonight,' Jessica admitted. 'Why isn't he married? Nice men usually get snapped up.'

'Laziness, I think. He has a comfortable home, is waited on hand and foot, has plenty of money for his interests and hobbies, and he only has to snap his fingers to get a girlfriend. Marriage would be a commitment. I think he prefers to play the field.'

'There, that's the lot. Thank you for your help, Jessica.'

Jessica would have liked to talk about Ian Grantly for a while longer, but a glance at the wall clock told her it was late.

She looked round for her bag and car keys.

'It was a lovely party,' she said as she shrugged her arms into her coat. 'See you tomorrow at about eleven.'

Thinking Of Jessica

Ian Grantly let himself into his house as quietly as he could. But it was not quietly enough. A bedroom door opened on the landing above and his mother, in her housecoat and slippers, popped out like a fluffy pink bird from a cuckoo clock.

'Did you have a nice evening, darling?' she asked from the top of the stairs.

'Quite good,' said Ian. 'Nothing special. The usual kind of party.' He wasn't getting into a discussion with his mother about who had been there and so on. He wanted to think about the evening quietly, on his own. And he certainly wasn't going to mention Jessica.

'Can I get you anything? A drink? Something to eat?'

'Nothing, Mother, thank you. Go back to bed. I'll see you in the morning.'

'Very well. Goodnight, darling.' She

blew him a kiss and returned to her room.

The drawing-room was in complete darkness. Feeling his way past small tables and large plants, Ian reached his favourite armchair, switched on the table-lamp at the side, and flung himself into the chair.

He leaned back and closed his eyes. Jessica Lawrence. Shiny hair like silky chocolate and long legs like . . .

He got up and crossed the room to a sideboard and poured himself a small whisky, then returned to his chair.

'Jessica Lawrence,' he muttered. 'I shall see you again whether you like it or not.' He took a sip of the whisky. 'But why?' he asked himself. 'Why do I want to see her again?' He knew plenty of girls just as pretty. What was so special about her?

She was bright, sassy, to use an American word, but she had a vulner-ability that appealed to him. The way her eyes had shone with the tears she was trying so hard to hold back had twisted his heart.

Her fiancé must be a fool to let such a girl go.

'I'd like to wring his neck,' he muttered. 'If I ever meet him he'd better look out.'

He leaned his head back and closed his eyes again. What did Jessica really feel about the brute? If she didn't want him back, there'd be a chance for someone else. Someone who'd really love and appreciate her. Someone like Ian Grantly.

He smiled ruefully into the darkened room. What about his resolution not to get serious about a girl? Not to spoil his comfortable, basically selfish life with the need to consider someone else.

Of course, she might refuse him. She was adamant that she wanted nothing more to do with men.

He stood up and switched out the light. He'd never had any problem attracting girls. Jessica was different. She seemed impervious to his charm. He would have to work carefully.

Jessica awoke with tears on her cheek. Late spring sunshine crept through the gaps at the edges of the window blind. She reached for her little bedside clock. Seven thirty. Still early. She could laze for a while.

She brushed away the tears with her fingers. Tears! Had she been crying in her sleep? Then her dream came back with a clarity she didn't desire.

She was waiting at the altar in her beautiful white silk wedding-dress. The air was scented with flowers. The church was full; the organ played softly. But where was Gregory? She had been waiting for hours, refusing to leave, tears streaming down her face. Then she'd woken up.

She reached under her pillow for a tissue and blew her nose. She refused to waste any more tears on Gregory.

She swung her legs out of bed and switched on the little electric kettle on a table in the corner, and raised the blind while the water heated. The garden of the small guesthouse where she was staying was bathed in early-morning sunshine. It was restful to drink a cup of tea looking out at the flowers. She watched the blackbirds searching diligently for breakfast delicacies amongst the fallen leaves and under the bushes.

Her thoughts went back to the evening before. Ian Grantly. He was a pleasant thought. What a shame Gregory hadn't turned up at the party to see her in the arms of such a handsome man.

Under the shower, she remembered again the scent of his cinnamon aftershave. She smiled to herself. He had been most persistent. But she wondered whether her lukewarm attitude might have cooled his ardour and whether she'd see him again.

'Do I want to see him again?' she asked herself as she began to dress. 'No, I don't. However attractive he is, I've finished with men. You can't trust them. From now on, my painting is the most important thing in my life.'

After a leisurely breakfast, she packed her painting and photography equipment into her car and drove the short distance to Hilly's house. Windows were open, which probably meant Mrs Dexter was hard at work, but there was no sign of Hilly. Jessica took her painting stool from the car and for half an hour tried various positions in front of the house, studying it for the view that appealed most.

The house had been built in the nineteen-thirties, a conventional between-the-wars residence, but its red brick walls were softened by a luxuriant growth of vivid green creeper. The windows were diamond-paned and glinted in the sunshine.

It was a large mock-Tudor building with the usual protruding white painted section ornamented with black beams, but with many interesting features that Jessica hoped to incorporate into her painting. She loved the curved bay windows at one side and the long sloping roof reaching across the garages on the other. Hilly's family loved it, and Hilly felt that a painting of the house for her mother to hang in her villa in Italy would be the perfect present.

Jessica took a frame from her box of painting equipment and held it up to her eyes, turning it this way and that. The little square cut out of a piece of card concentrated her vision and masked off areas of the scene, enabling her to decide how much of the house she would paint and from what angle.

The early morning haze had disappeared. The light was clearer. Jessica returned to the car and collected her camera. She needed many views and details of the house to enable her to complete the painting at home.

She was replacing the camera in the boot of the car when a voice behind her made her jump.

'Good morning, busy bee. You're up early.'

She spun round. 'Ian! What are you doing here?'

As handsome as she remembered, he was smiling as if sure of a friendly welcome. 'I said I'd be in touch.'

'You said you'd phone.'

'Yes, well, if I'd phoned, I'd only have heard you. This way I can see you, too.'

Jessica flushed. 'I haven't time for silly banter, I have work to do.'

'May I watch?'

'Do you think I can concentrate while you're watching me?'

'OK, I'll go. But only if you promise to have dinner with me tonight.'

Jessica gave a little chuckle. 'I suppose if I argue, you'll stay all morning.'

He opened his mouth to speak again but she forestalled him. 'Thank you, I'd like dinner tonight.'

He beamed. 'Really? That's wonderful. I'll pick you up about eight.'

Before she could move, he took her in his arms and danced her round the nearest tree. Eventually she managed to pull herself free.

'Don't be an idiot, someone will see.'

Someone had. Hilly emerged from

the side of the house. 'What on earth are you two doing?'

'I'm trying to carry out my commission,' said Jessica. 'I don't know what he's supposed to be doing.'

'Coffee time?' Ian asked hopefully.

'Don't give him coffee, we'll never be rid of him,' Jessica pleaded.

Hilly shooed him down the drive.

'See you tonight,' he called to Jessica.

'Tonight?' Hilly turned to her friend. 'Are you going out with him?'

'Just for dinner,' Jessica admitted. 'I had to agree or he'd still be here now. He won't take no for an answer.'

'Lock the car and come inside,' said Hilly. 'You can have some coffee.'

* * *

In the bright yellow and black kitchen, the girls perched on stools at the breakfast bar.

'I wonder whether I should warn you about Ian,' Hilly mused.

'Warn me? Is he dangerous?'

'Of course not, but he's flippant. He takes very little seriously. His work, of course, but very little else.' Hilly took a biscuit barrel from the cupboard and placed it between them.

'What does he do?'

'He trained as an accountant but now he runs his late stepfather's business. Does very well, I believe.'

'I can't see him as a businessman.'

'The firm is the only thing he's serious about,' said Hilly. 'Otherwise he's a sort of butterfly flitting here and there with lots of interests and no intention of settling down.'

'And dozens of girlfriends, I suppose.'

'Well — probably. But nobody special. He needs someone sensible to take him in hand.'

'Don't look at me.' Jessica added cream to her coffee and stirred it slowly. 'I'm not looking for a replacement for Gregory.'

'What made Gregory change his mind?' Hilly asked. 'I don't mean to pry,' she added quickly, 'but from what you've told me, plans for the wedding are well advanced.'

Jessica bit her lip. 'My dress is hanging in the wardrobe in my mother's spare room. The hotel is booked. The invitations have been ordered. So yes, you could say plans are well advanced.'

'He decided he isn't ready for marriage.' Jessica picked up her mug and sipped the coffee.

'Oh Jessica,' Hilly put a hand on her arm. 'What are you going to do?'

'I'm not going to beg him to come back to me, that's for sure.' Jessica brushed away the tears that began to fill her eyes.

'Do you still love him?' Hilly asked quietly.

Jessica considered.

'Do you know,' she said after a few minutes, 'I don't think I do. There's a cold lump in my stomach when I think of him. All my feelings for him have frozen and I don't think they'll melt.' She wiped her eyes. 'I'll get back to work now, if you don't mind. I want to do as much as possible before you go back to Italy in case I have any questions.'

Hilly smiled. 'Will you have lunch in the garden with me when I get back from the shops?'

'Of course. I'd like that.'

* * *

For the next two hours, Jessica worked busily. The house was on a secluded road, so there was no disturbance from traffic. The day was sunny but not too bright. The air was soft. Totally engrossed, Jessica photographed and sketched and made notes of colours and flowers.

She was still working hard when Hilly returned.

'Have a break,' she called. 'I'm going to make lunch. Don't be long.'

The girls ate sliced chicken and salad under a spreading oak tree in the middle of the lawn.

'I used to have a tree house up there.'

29

Hilly looked up into the dark branches above her. 'The tree is so dense you could hardly see it.'

'Sounds fun,' said Jessica. 'What a pity it's gone, we could have had our lunch up there today.'

Hilly looked down at her rounded figure. 'I'm not the shape for climbing trees any more,' she said with a laugh. She reached down into the freezer box beside her and took out two meringues covered with cream and chocolate shavings. 'And I shan't ever be again if I continue to eat treats like this. But I do so love it.' She handed a cake to Jessica.

'I'm not sure I should. I'm going out for a meal tonight,' Jessica reminded her. 'This might fill me up too much.'

'We'll walk briskly round the garden when you've eaten it. You can burn up the calories.'

The garden was an artist's palette of colours and a perfumery of scents.

'I could wander round here all day.' Jessica breathed deeply. 'It's so beautiful. But I have work to do.'

'Me too,' said Hilly reluctantly. 'Mother has given me a list of books to take out to her. We have a dozen bookcases so finding them will be a long job.'

They separated and Jessica returned to her sketchpad. As she picked up a charcoal stick, a thought struck her. They hadn't mentioned Ian once. She'd missed her chance to find out more about him.

Oh well, I have this evening to do that, she thought, and felt a little frisson of excitement at the idea. Getting to know Ian Grantly might be a pleasurable experience.

When she'd packed for her week painting Hilly's house, she hadn't imagined a need for evening clothes. Hilly had invited her to the party some time ago, so she'd brought her new dress, but the rest of her clothes were casual.

As she replaced all her painting equipment in the car, she experienced a feeling of panic. What could she wear that evening? Mentally she reviewed the contents of her suitcase and came up blank.

The small town of Breverton was only ten minutes away. She would have to go shopping. With a sigh, she steered the car out into the road. She didn't really feel like shopping. It was something she preferred to do when she had more time.

But she was in luck. The first shop she entered had a wide range of tops, tee-shirts and blouses. She flicked along the rail. Nothing too fancy, something classic, she decided.

She chose a white silk shirt with deep cuffs. Just the thing to go with her black trousers, smart but not too dressy. A brightly figured pashmina over one shoulder would lift the outfit and match her red, high-heeled shoes.

Later, surveying herself in the wardrobe mirror in her bedroom, she felt quite cheered by the result and when Ian's car pulled up outside she went to meet him with a brightly welcoming smile.

He nodded in approval at her appearance. 'Very nice too.'

★　★　★

His silver sports car was narrow and their shoulders pressed together as they sped along country lanes and eventually swung into the car park of an old black and white inn. Jessica tried to pretend she wasn't aware of his nearness but his wicked smile showed that he knew she was. He led the way across the car park to the heavy, nail-studded door under the swinging sign of the Green Feather.

They entered the black panelled bar. Though it was a summer evening, a fire burned brightly in the wide stone fireplace.

'Where would you like to sit?' asked Ian.

'Where I can see the fire,' she answered. 'I like to watch the flames.'

Ian gave her his crinkly smile. 'I can't believe you're here, that you agreed to come out with me.'

'Well, as you said, I had to eat tonight.'

They ate pub food, but fresh and well cooked. They both chose home-made chicken and mushroom pie.

'So much better than those horrible little individual ones that are all pastry,' Ian commented.

Jessica agreed when she tried the pie which contained large chunks of tender chicken, juicy mushrooms and a tasty gravy.

'Delicious!' She sat back, well satisfied, and looked across at Ian, wondering how many other girls he'd brought to this inn.

He read her thoughts. 'The Green Feather is only for my special friends,' he said. 'I don't want it to become so popular that I can't get in. Would you like a coffee?'

She watched the dancing flames of the fire while he went to order coffee. The inn had a timelessness that was restful.

She smiled up at him as he returned.

'You look more relaxed tonight,' he commented.

'It's a relaxing place.'

'It is. That's why I chose it. It's not really popular with the young crowd, so it never gets too noisy. So, tell me how you got started on your painting business? It's an unusual career.'

'When I finished college, I couldn't decide what aspect of art to follow. I saw an ad for an artist in a greetings card business not too far from home. I applied and got an interview.' She took a sip of her coffee. 'They examined my portfolio at length, said they were very, very good — and turned me down.'

Ian was looking at her thoughtfully. 'Do you know why?'

She shrugged. 'They had a few more people to see. Then I got a letter saying they'd found someone more suitable.'

'What was the name of the company?'

'I don't suppose you'd know it.'

He made no comment when she named them. There was silence for a few minutes then he said, 'So you decided to work for yourself?'

'Yes, though it was actually my father's idea. He subbed me for a while but the business took off quite rapidly. You wouldn't think many people would want a painting of their house, would you? But they do.'

'I think it's a wonderful idea. I'm sure my mother would like a painting of our house. We must discuss it some-time.'

Jessica glanced at the ponderous grandfather clock in the corner of the room. 'Goodness, is that the time? We should be going.'

'Can we do this again?' he asked. He put his hand over hers where it lay on the table and gave it a warm squeeze. Jessica heard warning bells but ignored them. She finished her coffee and stood up.

'I'll be going home soon, but I'm sure we can manage another evening if you like.'

'I certainly would like.' He took her elbow, rubbing his thumb up and down the inside of her arm as they walked to the car. She gave no sign of noticing but the caress gave her a tingling feeling up and down her arm.

As the car pulled out of the car park, she reflected that they hadn't once mentioned her engagement, and she was glad. She needed to do a lot of thinking about it, but didn't want to discuss it.

They were soon back at her guest house. Ian pulled up outside and sat looking at her. She was very conscious of his nearness. He made no move to touch her but kept his hands on the steering wheel.

'I've really enjoyed this evening,' he said.

'Me too. Thank you for taking me.'

'Will you be at Hilly's tomorrow?'

'I should think so. I must do what I can before she leaves.'

'May I call round? Perhaps she'll relent tomorrow and give me some coffee! Would you put in a good word for me?'

Jessica chuckled and made to open her door, but he put a hand on her arm. 'Jessica. I — ' But then he halted and gave a sigh. 'Never mind. Some other time. Wait, I'll open the door for you.'

In the shadow of the hedge beside the gate, he took both her hands and lifted them to his lips. His mouth burned against her skin.

'Goodnight, Jessica, and thank you.'

He was in his car and away before she could wonder whether she felt regret that his lips had found her fingers and not her mouth.

'Goodnight,' she whispered.

⋆　⋆　⋆

In the bedroom she quickly slipped into her nightdress and dressing gown. As she cleansed her face, she thought back over the evening. She was still engaged to Gregory, she supposed, but she had just enjoyed an evening with another man. And she had to confess, she'd enjoyed it more than any evening she'd spent with Gregory.

Gregory! Why had she got engaged to him? He was pleasant looking, had a good job and promised a secure future. But were any of these facts good enough reason for marriage if there was no love? For she knew now that she didn't love him; probably had never loved him. Her mother liked him. His mother liked Jessica. The mothers were best friends. And somehow the engagement had come about.

She remembered a conversation with her father one golden September day some months ago. They'd been working companionably collecting leaves and building a bonfire, and were sitting in the garden enjoying a cool drink. He had suddenly introduced the subject of the engagement.

'Do you want to get married, poppet?'

'Why do you ask?'

He had looked thoughtful. 'I've been watching you and Gregory together. You don't look to me like a couple in love. If you feel this engagement is a mistake, say so. Better a bit of embarrassment now than an unhappy marriage.'

Jessica considered. It was not like her father to put forward an opinion so contrary to her mother's ideas.

'Mum thinks it's a wonderful idea,' she began. 'She thinks Gregory is perfect husband material.'

'And so does Susan,' he agreed, mentioning Gregory's mother. 'And I'm not disputing that. But that doesn't make it right for you. Do you want this engagement?'

Jessica tried another approach. 'Do you like Gregory?'

'He's a nice enough lad but I don't think he's right for you,' he said gruffly. 'Don't ask me why I think that, I just do.' He picked up their glasses from the garden table. 'Just think about it, that's all.'

Though it was painful, she forced herself to remember the evening when Gregory had dashed all her hopes. They'd been to a dance at the local hotel. The evening had been fun and they'd left the hotel laughing and joking together. They'd got into the car and Gregory, staring straight ahead, had said, 'Jessica, I have something to confess.'

His tone was so serious that she'd stopped laughing.

'I can't get married.'

'Can't get — can't get married? What do you mean?'

'Just that. I can't get married. I love you, you're a wonderful, beautiful girl, but I can't marry you.'

'But why not? What's happened? Have you met someone else?'

'No! No.' He took her hand. 'I can't explain it but every time I think of the wedding I feel cold, as if something dreadful is going to happen.'

'Something dreadful,' she echoed. 'Marriage to me is going to be something dreadful?'

'I don't mean that. I mean that I don't think I'm ready for marriage. If I was, there's no one I'd rather marry.'

'Thank you,' she said bitterly. She fastened her seatbelt. 'You'd better take me home.'

They parted at her door without a hug or a kiss.

'I suggest we say nothing to our parents just yet. You may come to your senses and all this can be forgotten.'

That had been two weeks ago. She and Gregory hadn't spoken since.

She heard the jingle of her mobile phone ringing. At this time? Puzzled, she rummaged in her handbag and pulled it out.

'Jessica! At last! I've been ringing all evening.'

'What's wrong, Mum?'

'Nothing's wrong. Well, I hope not anyway. Your father says I'm fussing unnecessarily, but I can't stop thinking about you and Gregory. Have you seen him since you went to — ?'

'No. I imagine he's as busy working as I am,' said Jessica evasively.

'You're only forty miles away. I should have thought you'd want to see each other. Is he all right? Susan's worried about him.'

Jessica paused, then said, 'Actually I haven't spoken to him.'

'Haven't spoken to him?' There was outrage in her mother's voice. 'But you're engaged! Susan says he won't tell her anything. We both feel you're keeping something from us.'

'Look, Mum, it's late. I'll be home soon and we can talk then. Give my love to Dad.' She switched off her phone with trembling hands. Was this how the next few weeks were going to be? Questions and reproach?

She climbed into bed and snuggled down under the soft covers. The situation would be embarrassing for the mothers, she knew, but she was glad she had discovered how Gregory felt now and not after they were married. But how did she feel? Furious, embarrassed, relieved? Relieved? Yes. And excited for the future.

An Invitation

'Don't you ever do any work?' Jessica asked, laughter in her voice. Ian looked offended. 'Actually I'm working now. I'm on my way to see a customer. I had to pass Hilly's house and it seemed rude not to call and see how you're getting on.' He lowered himself on to the garden seat and looked at her solemnly. 'So how *are* you getting on?'

She smiled. 'Perfectly well, thank you.'

'You've started painting then?' he asked with real interest.

'Mm. Background. Not very detailed yet.'

'D'you think Hilly would give me a coffee today?'

'No.'

'That's very definite. Why not?'

'Because she's out. She's gone to the dentist.'

'Ah. I don't suppose you'd come out

somewhere with me for a coffee?'

'You suppose right. I'm busy. What is it with you and coffee? Can't you go somewhere on your own? Perhaps your customer will give you one.'

He gave a deep theatrical sigh. 'OK, I get the message. I'll go.' He stood up to walk away, then turned back. 'Do you work on Saturdays?'

'That depends on whether I have anything else to do.'

'Then I have a suggestion: something else you can do this Saturday. You'll like it,' he said when she looked at him suspiciously. 'A picnic. Do you like walking? I know a lovely place near a river. We can walk and talk and eat. I'll bring the food.' He was standing close to her. 'Please say yes.'

She smiled up at him, very aware of his nearness. 'It sounds a lovely idea.'

He let out his breath in a rush. 'Phew, I didn't have to fight too hard this time. I shan't see you tomorrow, I'm going to London. But I'll pick you up on Saturday morning at ten. Is that OK?'

'I'll look forward to it. What can I bring?'

'Just yourself.' His face crinkled up into a smile. 'Au revoir.' He walked away down the drive, pausing halfway to give her a jaunty wave.

Jessica continued painting, humming softly to herself.

'You sound happy this morning. Did I see Ian's car turning out of the drive as I came up the road?' Hilly had appeared behind her.

'Yes. He called to invite me to a picnic on Saturday.'

'Indeed! Just the two of you?'

Jessica coloured. 'Yes. He thought we could go for a walk first.'

'He's getting keen,' said Hilly. 'What about you? After all, you're a free woman now.'

Jessica looked down at the finger on her left hand where her sapphire engagement ring had sparkled for a few months. It lay safely in her jewellery box until she could return it to Gregory.

'I'm not a free woman yet; not

officially. And Ian and I are just friends.'

'All right, I won't tease,' said Hilly. 'I'm pleased to see that Ian is taking your mind off — things. I'll go and make some lunch. I'm hungry and I'm sure you're ready for something.'

Jessica watched her retreating figure. Hilly was a dear. She'd become quite fond of her. But she would keep analysing Jessica's feelings. It's time I went back to my flat for a bit of peace, thought Jessica.

* * *

Saturday dawned a perfect early June morning. Jessica drew back the curtains and looked out at the sunlit garden, breathing a sigh of relief. No rain, not even a shower.

Ian was on time and looked with approval at her neat green shorts and tee shirt.

'I haven't any proper walking shoes with me,' she said, 'but these are comfy. You don't plan a ten-mile hike, I hope?'

'A gentle stroll by the river,' he said. 'Hop in and we'll be off.'

In half an hour, the river came into view. They were on high ground and below them it snaked away into the distance between wooded banks. They began to descend a hill and were soon driving on to a parking space at the side of the water.

'It's beautiful,' said Jessica. 'So peaceful. Look at those ducks. Just like a procession of little boats.'

'Walk first or eat first?' Ian asked.

'Walk. I want to enjoy the lovely scenery and the fresh air.'

She jumped from the car and tied her white pullover round her waist.

'I don't suppose I'll need it but it might be cool by the water.'

They strolled at a gentle pace that suited them both. After a while, he took her hand. She glanced at him but he was studying a moorhen on the opposite bank. She decided the gesture was one of companionship and was happy to leave her hand in his.

The far bank was edged with reeds and bullrushes. Tiny moorhens and sturdy ducks, colourful males in front and dull brown females behind, sallied in and out of the foliage.

'I wish we'd brought some bread for them,' said Jessica.

'We'll come again and feed them,' he said.

'I'll buy a loaf especially for them.'

'It's supposed to be stale bread,' she said reproachfully. 'It would be wrong to buy a fresh loaf just for ducks.'

'Why? Don't ducks deserve nice food?'

'You know what I mean.'

Ian released her hand and slipped an arm around her waist. She let it rest there for a minute then gently moved away. He looked down at her.

'I'm sorry. I keep forgetting you're engaged.'

Jessica gave a bitter little laugh. 'Am I? I don't know . . . '

'Why did you get engaged? You don't seem madly in love or devastated by your loss.'

When she didn't reply, he took her hand. 'I'm sorry, that was presumptuous of me.'

'It's all right. Perhaps it would help to talk. Sort out my feelings.' She was quiet for a moment then the words began to flow. She found it surprisingly easy to talk to him.

'We met at a party. Gregory didn't seem to be enjoying himself; he's not much of a mixer. We talked, and discovered that our mothers knew each other.'

'But you'd never met?'

'No. The families didn't know each other, just the mothers. They belonged to a craft club, making blankets and toys for disadvantaged children. He asked me out. We went to a concert. I'd never been to a classical concert before and I really enjoyed it. In return I took him to art galleries. We shared our interests.'

'And your mothers were pleased. I think I can guess what's coming next. It explains why you seem rather lukewarm about this relationship.'

Do I come over as lukewarm, she wondered?

'Naturally the mothers were pleased,' she went on. 'My mother thought Gregory would be perfect for me: steady, serious and with a good job. His mother liked me. She was relieved that I enjoyed cooking. Her precious son would be well fed.'

'What about the fathers?'

'Gregory's father works away a great deal. I've only met him two or three times. My father was concerned. He wasn't too keen on Gregory. He thought he was spoilt and selfish.' She stopped suddenly. 'Look, a kingfisher!'

They gazed, entranced, at the beautiful jade green and orange bird, poised on a branch which bent over the river.

'He's looking for fish. Watch,' Ian whispered as the bird swooped into the water and emerged with a small silver fish. It swallowed the wriggling creature and prepared to dive again. But a sudden squawk from the reeds startled it and it streaked along the river surface and disappeared.

Jessica turned dancing eyes to her companion.

'Wasn't that exciting! It's rare to see a kingfisher, I believe.'

'I've never seen one before, though there are supposed to be quite a few along here. You must have brought me luck.'

They walked on, looking out for more kingfishers, but were disappointed.

'Are you hungry now?' asked Ian. 'Shall we go back for our picnic?'

Jessica nodded. 'I could eat something now. It must be the fresh air.'

They returned to the car. Ian spread a rug on the grass close to the water and lifted a large picnic basket from the boot. His mother had sent a feast: egg mayonnaise, ham patties, salad, cold chicken, trifles and a range of drinks.

'Mother loves picnics,' he explained, 'but she hates sandwiches and buns, hence the range of delicacies.'

'It all looks fantastic,' said Jessica, tucking in.

Ian opened a bottle of chilled white wine and poured them each a glass.

'You'll have to drink most of this; I'm driving.'

Jessica leaned back against a tree, sipping her wine. 'What a perfect way to spend an afternoon,' she said softly.

'Did you finish telling me about Gregory? I think the kingfisher interrupted you.'

'There's not much more to tell. The mothers kept pushing us together. We just drifted into an engagement.'

'So what went wrong? Why did you break off the engagement?'

'It's gallant of you to think I broke it off, but the truth is, it was Gregory.' She bit her lip. 'I was dumped.'

He looked at her in amazement. This lovely girl! Gregory must be mad, he thought, and said as much.

'He said marriage was too much of a commitment. He wasn't ready for it.' Jessica pressed her lips together to stop them from trembling.

'Then why did he get engaged?'

'I told you, the mothers were pushing it. I don't think either of us thought it through. Goodness, doesn't that make us sound feeble?'

He was silent, thinking. Then he said, 'My mother likes her own way. She likes to influence me, suggest what she thinks is best. But she'd never push me into marriage.'

'What about you?' she asked. 'We've talked a lot about me. What about your love life?'

'My love life?' He smiled ruefully. 'I suppose you could say I'm afraid of commitment, too. Perhaps most men are. I've had several girlfriends, all nice girls, but I've never found the right one. How can you decide that someone is so right for you that you'll never change your mind? And I wouldn't want to change my mind. I believe marriage is for life.'

'I suppose you just know,' said Jessica after a pause for thought. 'You don't have to think about it, you just know.' She gazed at him and this time it was his turn to colour and look down.

'I like my freedom,' he admitted. 'I don't want to feel tied down. I like girls very much.' He gave her his crinkled grin. 'But as friends. I believe you and I could be good friends, don't you?'

She nodded, but wondered what he was really trying to tell her. Maybe he was saying, don't get too close, don't see me as a replacement for Gregory. But so far he'd made all the running. The picnic was his idea.

'Enough of this serious talk.' Ian jumped up and began to pack the picnic basket. Jessica made to help, but he waved her back. 'I can manage. You stay there and look for kingfishers.'

When he came back from stowing the basket in the car, he shook out the rug and threw himself down.

'Come and join me,' he urged.

'I wouldn't see any kingfishers from there.'

'Never mind the kingfishers.' His voice was sleepy. 'Come and have a snooze.'

Jessica didn't answer and remained

resolutely where she was. A bee droned gently in the clover at her feet. The sun was warm on her face. Her eyelids began to close . . .

She woke ten minutes later to see Ian lying on his stomach, watching her. 'You'd have been more comfortable here for your sleep,' he said.

'I wasn't asleep,' she retorted. 'I was just resting my eyes. It's very hot.'

Ian went to the car and returned with two small bottles of orange juice. 'They're nice and cold. They've been in the coolbox.'

Jessica drank thirstily. 'Just what I wanted.' She glanced at her watch. 'Goodness, it's half past four already. We should be getting back.'

'Why? It's early,' he protested. 'You don't want to go back yet, do you? Are you bored with me?' He put on a dejected expression.

Jessica laughed. 'Of course not. I've had a lovely day. But I must be up early in the morning and I have things to get ready tonight.'

'May I ask where you're going tomorrow?'

'Home. To my flat. I must collect post and wash a few clothes. I want a whole day there.'

'Could I come with you?' he asked hopefully.

'What, and sit about all day while I do my washing?' she asked with a laugh. 'I'm sure you have more interesting ways to spend your time.'

'So I have to stay here on my own and wait for your return.' He picked up the car rug, shook it and folded it.

'I think that would be the best idea,' she said solemnly.

They climbed into the car. As she reached to put on her safety belt, her bare arm brushed his and a tingle ran down to her fingertips. She had to stop herself saying, 'All right, you can come with me.' The idea of another day in his easy company was a great temptation.

Instead she said, 'Thank you for a lovely day, Ian. And thank your mother for the delicious picnic.'

He took her hand and gently squeezed it. 'Thank you for coming,' he said.

★   ★   ★

After Hilly's spacious house, her flat looked tiny. But it was home, comfortable and familiar. Jessica made herself a cup of tea, gathered up a pile of post from behind the door and settled herself in an armchair.

There were two bills, a letter from her sister Claire in Canada, another letter with an unfamiliar postmark and two enquiries from prospective clients. She put those on one side to telephone later and opened Claire's letter.

It started as all Claire's letters did:

When are you coming to see me? I miss you dreadfully. I can get you painting commissions here, I'm sure.

Jessica smiled. She missed Claire too and hadn't yet seen the little niece who was named after her. She let the letter fall into her lap and gazed out of the window. Would it be a good idea to leave the country for a while and visit Claire?

She would get away from Gregory and the difficulties with the mothers. But what about Ian? Their relationship would come to an end before it had even started.

Relationship? What relationship? He'd made it plain he wanted no commitment. Good friends, he'd said. But perhaps if she went away, he'd miss her enough to —

But what was she thinking? She'd already decided her painting was to come first in her life. Friendship with Ian would have to be enough.

She put Claire's letter back into its envelope and laid it on one side to read again later. Then she picked up the envelope with the unknown postmark and opened it. There were two sheets of writing paper inside.

Dear Jessica, it began. *We said we'd keep in touch but we haven't, have we? How are you getting on? I'm teaching. Not a very exciting career after all our plans but perhaps things will change one day.*

Jessica turned over the page and looked at the signature. *Caro.* Caro Pearson. One of her friends at art college. There had been four of them who did everything together from visiting art galleries to entering competitions and helping each other with their projects. They'd called themselves the Four Jacks after the initial letters of their names: Jessica, Anya, Caro and Kit.

'We must keep in touch!' they'd vowed when they left, but like all such vows, it was difficult to keep. Jessica really had meant to write or phone her friends, but somehow days and weeks and months had passed and she'd found her time filled by her career and her plans with Gregory.

The others must have been just as busy because this was the first communication she'd received from any of them. She studied the letter again.

I ran into Anya the other day and we decided it's time the Four Jacks got together again, Caro went on. *What do you think of a short break together in Cornwall? Anya has written to Kit and I'm writing to you. If we all agree, we'll make plans. Do say you'll come. It'll be fun!*

Jessica read the letter through again. Well, why not? She deserved a holiday. Cornwall! She hadn't been there for years. She gazed into space seeing again blue-green waves edged with white foam, rocks and sandy coves, and picture postcard villages. Yes, she'd like that.

* * *

For the next hour she worked solidly, washing and ironing, and repacking her suitcase with clean clothes. This time,

61

she added another dress ready for any more evening invitations.

In her studio she sorted out some brushes and more white paint. She seemed to get through more tubes of white paint than any other colour.

She was just opening a cupboard door and reaching for another sketch-pad when the ringing of the doorbell startled her. Who — ?

For one ridiculous moment, she imagined that Ian had followed her. Then, like a douche of cold water, she realised who it must be. She opened the door to find Gregory standing there, his expression wary.

'I saw your car,' he said. 'I was driving past and — '

Without speaking, she held open the door and he walked past her into the little sitting-room.

'I didn't know you were coming back today,' he began.

'Why should you?' Her voice was icy. 'I had no reason to tell you.'

'Jessica, please don't be bitter.'

She was so outraged she was unable to speak for a moment.

'Don't I have a right to be bitter? Bitter and angry. Everything was ready for our wedding and you changed your mind. How am I supposed to feel?'

'Can't we discuss things calmly? May I sit down?' Without waiting for her reply, he sank into the nearest armchair.

Jessica realised she wasn't going to be able to get rid of him easily, and reluctantly took a seat opposite.

'Have you told your mother?' she asked.

He had the grace to look shame-faced. 'No.'

'Why not?'

'Because my mother phoned to say that yours is upset. She thinks something's wrong and doesn't know what. Have you told yours?'

'Not yet,' she admitted.

'If we wait for a while,' he began, 'I might . . .'

'What? Change your mind and agree to marry me? If you think I'm going to sit around waiting for you to make a definite decision about our marriage, you can forget it. The more I think about it, the more I agree that you were right. We should give up the whole idea.'

'So why haven't you told your parents?'

'It hasn't been convenient. I've been working away. It's not the sort of thing you can explain over the phone. I'll tell them soon.'

'Your father won't be sorry. He never liked me.'

'Are you surprised? And he was right, wasn't he?'

'I don't think this discussion is really getting us anywhere,' said Gregory, standing up. 'Perhaps we can meet again when you're feeling more reasonable.'

'When I'm — ' Jessica was speechless. 'I'm leaving in a few hours. I don't know when I'll be back, and I certainly won't be in what you call a reasonable frame of mind.' She marched to the door and wrenched it open.

'Are you seeing your parents?' Gregory asked, following her.

'They're away. I'll talk to them when I come back for good. You may do as you like.'

'Jessica — ' His voice softened. 'This is silly. Can't we — ?'

She looked at him. How could she ever have seen anything in him, anything attractive enough to agree to an engagement? He was shorter than Ian. His eyes didn't sparkle; his smile didn't crinkle.

Guiltily, she realised it was unfair to compare him to Ian, but she couldn't help it. And he failed on all counts. She took a deep breath.

'Goodbye, Gregory. Oh, you'd better take this with you, I shan't be needing it . . . ' She marched into her bedroom, snatched up her jewel box and removed the engagement ring which she dropped into Gregory's hand. He closed his fingers over it without a word and left the flat.

When he'd gone, she collapsed into a chair, shaking. She hated rows and this had been a prize one. Time to leave.

* * *

Back at the guesthouse, she unpacked her case and hung up her clothes. Then she prepared her equipment for the next day.

It was only six-thirty. Still early. She set out the food she'd brought for her evening meal, but realised she wasn't hungry. Perhaps Hilly would like some company for the evening.

The silver sports car parked in front of the house showed that Hilly already had company. With mixed feelings, Jessica rang the doorbell.

Hilly was delighted to see her. 'You're back nice and early. Come in. You can't spend a long evening on your own. Ian's here, but of course you can see that.' She gestured towards his car as she closed the door.

Ian was leaning back comfortably in an armchair but he jumped to his feet as she entered.

'Jessica! What a nice surprise.' He fussed in a very satisfying way and

Jessica's feelings, wounded by Gregory, were gentled.

Ian gave her a wide smile. 'How did you enjoy your day at home?'

'It was a busy day, not an enjoyable one, washing, ironing, packing, and sorting out my art supplies. Then Gregory turned up and we had another row.' She took a sip of the wine Hilly had poured for her.

'He accused me of being bitter,' she said. 'What else should I be?'

'What a shame,' said Hilly. 'You go back for just one day and there's an unpleasant scene.'

Jessica put down her wine glass and picked up her handbag to look out the letter from Caro.

'Never mind,' she said, 'something nice happened, too.'

'That letter?' asked Ian.

'Mm. It's from Caro Pearson, a friend from art college.' She told them briefly about the Four Jacks. 'So the suggestion is that we have a long weekend together in Cornwall. Renew our friendship and do a bit of painting and sketching together.'

'What a lovely idea.' Hilly was enthusiastic. 'It would be a shame to lose contact with such good friends.'

'Where in Cornwall shall you go?' asked Ian.

'Somewhere on the north coast. Caro's parents have a seaside cottage in a village there.'

'Lucky girl,' he said. 'The north coast is very exciting. And of course, St Ives is a wonderful place for artists.'

'You've made up my mind for me. I hadn't quite decided.'

'Would you like me to come with you as a bodyguard?' Ian asked innocently.

'We're big girls. No escorts required,' she said, laughing.

'Pity. I should love a break in Cornwall.' He stood up. 'I must go now. I only popped in to collect some CDs I loaned Hilly for the party.'

Left alone, the girls smiled at each other.

'He's really smitten,' said Hilly. 'He'd

love to go with you to Cornwall if you'd let him. But he'll still be here when you get back,' she said, 'and probably even more keen!'

A Gentle Warning

Two days later, the painting of Hilly's house was finished. Jessica set it up on an easel in front of the house and inspected it for a long time.

Then she gave a sigh. It was as perfect as she could make it.

She went into the house and found Hilly sitting on the floor surrounded by piles of books and holding a long typewritten list.

Jessica gave her a smile. 'It's finished.'

'Oh I must see it!' Hilly pulled herself to her feet with the aid of a chair. 'I'm so stiff. I've been sitting here for almost an hour.'

The two girls studied the painting, Jessica waiting anxiously for the verdict, Hilly with quiet concentration. At last Hilly turned to her with a satisfied smile.

'I love it and so will Mother. I can't

thank you enough.'

'It needs a frame now,' said Jessica. 'Will I take it to the framers or would you prefer to do it yourself?'

'Let's go together,' said Hilly. 'We can have tea and cakes while we're out.'

'Never one to miss a chance of a cake,' teased Jessica.

'Let's go now,' Hilly decided. 'I'm tired of these books. Why Mother wants such a long list I can't imagine.'

Jessica carefully carried the painting to the car. 'I haven't done much to it today, so there are only a few tiny areas of paint still wet. We'll ask them to wait until it's quite dry before framing it.'

It didn't take long to choose a frame, and the framer promised to have it ready in a week.

They entered the patisserie in a happy mood.

'This is my treat. Two large cream cakes to celebrate the picture.'

'When are you returning to Italy?' Jessica asked when they were settled at a corner table.

'Next month, I think.' Hilly applied herself to the large meringue she had chosen.

'And will you take the picture with you or send it?'

'Oh, send it. I think that'll be safer than if I was responsible for it.'

'Does your mother know or will it be a surprise?'

'A surprise . . . if I arrive before the painting does. I can't trust her not to open it if I'm not there.' She finished her cake and sat back with a sigh. 'That was delicious. I could eat another. But I shan't,' she said hastily when Jessica gave her a severe look.

'Changing the subject, when are you seeing Ian again?'

Jessica shrugged. 'I don't know. We haven't made any plans.'

'What about when you go home? Will you still see him then?'

Jessica was silent, thinking. 'There's nothing between Ian and me,' she said at last. 'There's no reason why we should see each other.'

'He's getting very interested in you,' said Hilly.

'I don't think so. He likes to play the field. I'm just a novelty for a while. There are plenty of other girls about. He'll soon forget me.'

'Will you go home soon, now you've finished my picture?'

'I've got another commission in the area, so I think I'll stay on at the guest-house for a week.'

'Another commission? How exciting. Is it a house?'

'How did I guess you two would be here?' asked a breezy voice.

Startled, the girls looked up to see Ian beaming down at them.

'You need to be careful,' he warned Jessica. 'Too much of Hilly's company and you'll become — um, curvy like her.'

'Can't we do anything without you turning up like a bad penny?' Hilly asked with mock annoyance.

As Ian pulled up a chair, a waitress appeared as if by magic and he ordered a pot of tea.

'How do you do it?' asked his cousin.

'Do what?'

'Get a waitress to appear the moment you sit down. We had to wait.'

'It's his natural charm,' said Jessica, and he gave her his wicked smile.

'Oh, you noticed. Now, what were we talking about?'

'We were talking about Jessica's next commission. She's finished the house.'

'I must call and see it,' he said.

'It's at the framer's.'

'Then I'll call in and ask to see it there.'

'He has an answer for everything, doesn't he?' Jessica said, picking up the coffee pot.

'So what's your new commission?' Ian turned to her with interest. 'Another house?'

'No. It's strange — well, rather sweet, really. It's a gateway. A very nice elderly couple have asked me to paint the gateway where they used to meet when they were young. It's the gateway to a field.

'They told me the whole story. Her father disapproved of the match, so they each used to go for a walk at three o'clock every Sunday afternoon for about half a mile out of the village, and meet at this gateway to a cornfield. I've been to see it. It's very pretty with hills in the distance.'

'That's so romantic,' said Hilly.

'It's also quite sad,' said Jessica. 'Someone bought the field for house-building last year.'

'So they want a picture to remember it as it was,' said Ian. 'Will you use oils or watercolour?'

'Watercolour. It's softer. More suit-able for the subject.'

They were silent, each thinking of the story.

'They must have got together despite the father,' Hilly decided.

'He died suddenly two years after they met, so they were free to marry,' Jessica explained.

'So when shall you start it?' Ian asked.

'Next week. I have to do some

clothes shopping for my little holiday with my friends. And of course we have to meet to make plans. I'm going up to London tomorrow for that.'

Ian looked at his watch and gasped. 'Look at the time. I'm supposed to be at the other side of town in ten minutes. What d'you mean by keeping me talking like this?'

'Did we *ask* you to join us?' Hilly asked, teasing.

Ian picked up his briefcase, and blew them each a kiss. They watched as he wound his way through the tables and out the door.

'He doesn't get any better,' said Hilly.

The cafe was beginning to fill up. 'We'd better go,' Jessica said, looking around at the crowded tables. 'We've been here a long time.'

'Let's go home and have a lazy afternoon in the garden,' suggested her friend. 'I'm fed up with sorting books.'

'I really should sort out my paints,' Jessica protested half-heartedly.

'Do that this evening,' Hilly cajoled.

'It's a beautiful afternoon. Why waste it indoors?'

* * *

The Four Jacks met at the restaurant of the Strickland Hotel in London. Jessica and Caro arrived at the same time and fell into each other's arms.

'You haven't changed a bit,' Jessica exclaimed.

'Nor you,' Caro returned. 'Isn't it amazing!' They both laughed with the pleasure of being together again. 'How long is it? Four years?'

'I don't believe it. It seems like four months. And yet it's been too long. This was a wonderful idea. I can't wait to see the others.'

'There's Kit!' Jessica waved excitedly. 'Kit! Over here!'

Smiling widely, Kit made her way through the tables towards them. All through college Kit had worn black from head to toe with large and colourful necklaces as the only relief. Jessica was amused to see she still dressed this way.

Kit gave her friends exuberant hugs, and once released Caro looked eagerly around the restaurant. As the tallest of the four she could see over the crowd and soon spotted Anya coming into the room.

'Anya! Anya!' She waved her hands above her head and Anya, looking relieved, headed towards them.

'Isn't this a super idea?' she said, grinning at her friends.

'Just what I said,' said Jessica, giving her a kiss. 'Anya, you look fantastic. Have you lost weight? It suits you.'

Anya gave a self-satisfied smile. 'I did it for a purpose. I'm getting married next year.'

There were congratulations all round while Anya produced photographs of her fiancé, then Caro said, 'Let's get some drinks and catch up on the gossip. We can eat later.'

Once they had got a round of drinks and were seated at a table in a corner of the crowded restaurant, Caro said,

'Right. Careers up till now. What are we all doing? I'm teaching. It pays the rent until my undoubted talent as a potter is recognised. I've done a few exhibitions, sold some pots, but not enough to give up the day job.'

'I'm doing window displays,' Kit said, taking her turn. 'I've set up my own company, small but growing. What about you, Anya?'

'Illustration work,' said Anya. 'Mostly children's books. I love it.'

'You always had a knack for drawing animals,' Jessica remembered.

'And what about you, Jessica?' asked Caro.

'I paint houses,' Jessica told them with a laugh.

They looked at her blankly.

'Houses? You did an art degree to paint houses? Oh, Jess . . . '

'I mean people pay me to have a painting done of their house. Usually for a present. It's getting to be quite popular.'

They all laughed, sharing the joke.

'I couldn't quite see you in overalls with ladders and tins of white gloss!' Kit spluttered.

The next hour passed happily as they caught up on each other's lives. Apart from Anya, none of them was in a serious relationship. Jessica didn't mention Gregory. It would have been too embarrassing to admit she'd effectively been left at the altar.

'You mean there's no one at all in your life?' Caro pressed. 'All work and no play, etcetera . . . '

'Well . . . I did meet someone at a party recently.'

'Come on, tell all,' they chorused. It was just like the old days.

'There's nothing to tell. We got on well, went out to dinner, talked.'

'Sounds promising,' said Anya. 'Where is he now? Doesn't he mind you going away?'

'He could hardly mind. We're not an item.'

The waitress began to hover. 'Are you ready to order now?'

Once their orders were taken they discussed their plans.

'Where in Cornwall are we going?' Jessica asked.

'Port Gawain,' said Caro. 'It's a small village, but cute, and it has everything we need.'

'You mean a good inn for the evenings,' Kit said with a laugh.

'Two,' said Caro, 'and a cafe and a small general store.'

'Well, that's our stomachs taken care of,' Anya chipped in. 'What about the beach?'

'Small — a cove, actually. But it's sandy when the sea goes out and there's plenty of big flat rocks to lie on. We needn't stay in the cove — Cornwall has plenty of beaches.'

'Is there room in your parents' cottage for all of us?' asked Jessica.

'My parents won't be there, and there are two bedrooms and four beds so we'll manage very well.'

They smiled at each other in anticipation.

'Now we only have to settle on a date,' said Caro.

'I have a slight problem with that. I'm teaching so I can't take time off. But it's half term in two weeks if that would suit everyone.'

They were just agreeing that it would as their food arrived. Jessica raised her glass.

'To our holiday in two weeks,' she said.

'Our holiday,' they chorused.

* * *

'This is a very lonely road,' said Ian severely. 'Did you really think I would let you paint here on your own?'

She had come back from her date in London to find a message from him arranging to meet her when she went to look at the gateway she had been commissioned to paint. She gave him a quick sideways glance. Let me? She thought, but she said nothing. If Ian wanted to be protective, so be it. And it

82

was a lonely road.

He drew the car in close to a hedge and switched off the engine.

'It'll be safe enough there, I'm sure. It doesn't look as if many people use this road. Nothing's passed us yet.'

Jessica climbed out and stretched. A light breeze blew the fresh scent of grass and wild flowers towards them.

'The gateway is back there. Let's go and look at it . . . '

They strolled back a few yards.

'How do you know this is the right one?' he asked. 'There must be several gateways along this field.'

Jessica reached down into the hedge near the bottom of the gate and untied a red ribbon.

'There,' she said, triumphantly holding it up for him to see. 'They said they'd leave a marker.'

'What if someone had removed it?'

She went to the hedge on the other side of the gate and bent down.

'Here we are.' She waved another red ribbon. 'Back-up!'

He grinned and, taking them from her, retied them to the low branches. 'Just in case you forget which one it is next time.'

They leaned on the old wooden gate and looked across the fields to the hills beyond. Birds were searching amongst the stubble, squawking and arguing.

'It's the same gateway, but I wonder if it's the very same gate as well?' Jessica mused.

'I should think so. Gates like this were made to last. What exactly do they want in the picture?'

'They said they'd leave it to me.' She was studying the scene critically. 'I think I'll sit across the lane.' She pointed behind her. 'And paint what I can see from there. That way I can bring in the gate and everything beyond it.'

He nodded. 'Let's get your bag and easel out of the car. I'll take some photos for you. Will that help?'

'Oh, yes! Then I can do most of the painting in the studio.'

'Studio? Does that mean you plan to go home to finish it, then?'

'No. Hilly's summerhouse is serving as my studio while I'm here.' She reached into the boot and drew out her bag of sketching materials and an easel. Ian picked up her stool and his camera and they returned to the gate.

For half an hour they worked without stopping, Jessica sketching in the gate and the hedges, and the hills beyond, and putting a colour code on the sketch for future reference.

'I wonder if they'd like birds and stubble or some cows in the field?' she called to Ian. 'What do you think?'

He considered.

'I suppose it depends on how you are on drawing cows,' he decided. 'Anyway, there might not have been cows in the field when they were young. Perhaps you'd better ask.'

'I'll phone tonight.' Jessica returned to her sketching.

'I've taken plenty of shots,' he said after a while. 'D'you want to see?'

'Let's have a drink first. There's some pineapple juice in the car,' said Jessica.

They studied Ian's photographs. He'd snapped the gateway from every possible angle, close up and from a distance. Jessica was pleased.

'This'll be a great help,' she said, returning the camera. 'Perhaps I'll employ you permanently as my assistant.'

He gave her an intense look and she flushed, bending down to her box of charcoal to try to hide her confusion.

'Ten minutes more and we can go,' she said, applying the black stick skillfully.

Ian watched for a while in silence then broke off to take in the scene around them. He pointed to the hills in the distance.

'Look at that cloud formation above the peaks. Isn't it dramatic?'

She smiled. 'It will be in the picture,' she assured him, wondering whether he thought she hadn't noticed.

At last she put down her pencil and closed the box. 'That's enough for today. I can make a good start tomorrow.'

'I'll print out these photos when I get back and bring them over this evening,' Ian promised as they returned to the car and stowed her equipment in the boot.

★   ★   ★

'Let's have dinner on the terrace,' Hilly suggested as she and Jessica caught up on their day later on. 'It's a lovely evening. I'll put everything on trays — it's only salad — and we can carry them out.'

Hilly disappeared into the kitchen and Jessica wandered over to the window which looked out on to the front garden and the drive. A large black car was coming slowly towards the house.

'Hilly!' she called. 'There's a taxi drawing up outside.'

Hilly hurried in. 'A taxi? Who can it . . . Oh no! Mother!'

As Jessica watched, a plump, expensively-dressed woman emerged from the taxi and spoke to the driver.

'Where's my bag?' Hilly looked around the room distractedly. 'She never has money to pay taxi drivers.'

Grasping it from a side table, she hurried out.

Before Hilly could return and make any introductions, the large lady had swept into the room on a cloud of exotic perfume. She stopped when she saw Jessica and held out her hand. 'Ramona Penn. How do you do? I'm Hilly's mother.'

She was so grand that Jessica felt that perhaps she should curtsey.

'Jessica Lawrence,' she said. 'I'm a friend of Hilly's.'

Before either could say any more, Hilly returned.

'Ah, you've introduced yourselves,' she said. 'I thought you were in Italy,' she went on, addressing her mother. 'What are you doing here?'

'I live here,' said the authoress pertly. 'Or had you forgotten?'

'You know what I mean.' Jessica was surprised to see how flustered her normally placid friend had become.

Ramona Penn selected a chair and arranged herself elegantly in it.

'I had to pop over to London to see my agent. Some silly little — ' she flicked her fingers dismissively ' — complication. So I thought I'd call in and see you. I'm not staying, I'm getting a late flight up to Edinburgh this evening, to stay with Aunt Kirstie for a few days. Do you want to come?'

Hilly shook her head. 'No, thank you, it's too much of a rush. And besides, I have plenty to do here.'

Jessica had quietly eased herself into another chair. Now the older woman turned to her.

'Are you staying with Hilly?'

'No, I'm in a guesthouse not far away.'

Ramona turned to her daughter. 'If you have a friend visiting you, why is she in a guesthouse? We have plenty of bedrooms.'

'I'm not exactly visiting Hilly,' Jessica explained. 'I'm working in the area.'

'Working?'

'Jessica is an artist,' Hilly explained. 'She

paints houses and . . . things,' she ended lamely, not wanting to go into details.

'And what are you painting at the moment? I'd like to see it.'

'I've been painting the countryside round about,' Jessica said vaguely. 'I don't actually have any work here with me.' She knew it sounded weak and was glad when Hilly hurried to change the subject.

'Can I get you something to drink, Mother? Coffee, perhaps?'

'I'd love a nice English cup of tea,' said her mother after a moment's thought. 'It never tastes the same in Italy even though I take English tea back with me.'

'Perhaps it's the water,' Jessica began, when the sound of another car door being slammed on the drive made them all turn towards the window.

'Who is it now . . . ?' Jessica heard Hilly mutter.

'Aunt Ramona,' came a voice from the doorway, and Ian stood there holding a large, flat object. 'I was passing the framer's,' he said to Hilly, 'so I thought I'd pop in and see if the painting was ready.' He placed the object against the wall then turned to kiss his aunt.

'Lovely to see you, Auntie.'

'Would that be one of Miss Lawrence's paintings?' Ramona inquired.

Ian became aware of Hilly's frantic gestures from behind her mother's back and realised that he had given the game away. Jessica was amused to see that for once he was at a loss for words.

'I should very much like to see it,' Ramona said. 'Would you be a sweetie and unwrap it, Ian? I'm sure Miss Lawrence won't mind, will you, Miss Lawrence?'

It was the kind of request that couldn't be refused. Slowly, and with an apologetic grimace at the girls, Ian unwrapped the painting and propped it up where his aunt could study it.

'This is very good,' she pronounced at last. 'You didn't tell me about this,' she said, turning accusingly to Hilly.

'It was to have been a surprise,' the girl said sadly.

'I'm so sorry. I feel dreadful.' Ian put an arm around Hilly.

'It doesn't matter. I'll make some tea.'

'Let me help you.' Jessica hastily followed her friend. She had no desire to stay with Ian and his aunt.

'Come and sit by me,' they heard Ramona command her nephew as they left the room. 'Have you thought any more about marriage. It's time you settled down.'

'Poor Ian,' Jessica said with a smile. 'I think he's really afraid of your mother.'

'We're all afraid of her,' said Hilly. 'What she commands has to be done.' She gave Jessica a stiff little smile. 'Take that tray in, would you? I'll bring some cake and biscuits.'

Jessica was crossing the hall when Ramona's voice reached her: ' . . . eminently suitable. Don't let her slip through your fingers.'

'There are reasons why I can't — ' Ian began.

'Nonsense. She doesn't wear a ring so she's obviously free. What do you know about her?'

Colour flooded into Jessica's cheeks.

She couldn't walk in on that conversation. They were obviously talking about her.

Hilly came up behind her just then. 'What's wrong?'

'Nothing. It's just that — well, they seem to be talking about me.'

'Matchmaking, I'll bet,' hissed Hilly. 'She doesn't want me to marry, so she's working on Ian instead.'

She marched into the room, causing the conversation to stop abruptly.

Doesn't want her to marry? Jessica thought. Whatever can she mean? I must remember to ask her.

'When everyone was settled with tea and cake, Ramona turned to Jessica. 'So, you take commissions?' she began.

'Yes, when I can get them.' The girl smiled.

'Well, I shall give you one. I want you to come to Italy and paint my villa. It will be a companion piece to the one of this house.' She picked up a piece of cake and began to eat as if the matter was settled.

Jessica looked at Hilly and then at the famous authoress. 'But — Italy — ' she began.

'Have you any objections?' Ramona responded at once.

'No, of course not. I've always wanted to visit Italy.'

'Are you busy at the moment? Can you return with me?'

'Oh no. I'm sorry. I have several pieces to finish and I've promised a friend I'll paint her parents' cottage in Cornwall.'

'Well, perhaps it would be a rush for you to return with me,' Ramona conceded. 'But I want to see you in the near future, before the summer is over.' She stood up and straightened the skirt of her beautifully cut suit. 'Now I'll just take a quick look at the garden while Ian gets me a taxi.'

Jessica wondered why Ian didn't offer to take his aunt to the airport then realised that he probably didn't want another lecture on his marriage prospects.

When Ramona had gone, Ian began to apologise to Hilly again.

'I'm so stupid. You told me it was to be a surprise.'

'It doesn't matter,' Hilly insisted. 'And at least it's had one good outcome — Jessica has another commission. In Italy.' They both looked at Jessica.

'You'll go, of course,' said Ian. 'It's so beautiful there. The Villa Gardenia is right on the edge of the lake. It'll be a holiday at the same time.'

'It's a wonderful opportunity,' she admitted, 'but there are other things to settle first.'

They both knew she was thinking of her own mother — and Gregory.

Friendships Renewed

Jessica made an early start on her journey to Cornwall. Soon the morning coolness gave way to uncomfortable heat as the sun rose in the sky. The sun beat down on the roof of the car so that despite the air-conditioning, Jessica felt she was travelling in an oven.

Crossing the wide space of Bodmin Moor, she finally saw, to her relief, the sign pointing to Jamaica Inn. She swung off the road and was soon parking near the cobbled yard of the inn.

There was a welcome coolness inside the low-ceilinged building. Jessica thankfully drank a whole bottle of mineral water then ordered her favourite meal, their famous steak and ale pie. As she ate, she thought back to the dinner she'd had with Ian at the Green Feather.

An hour later, back in the car, comfortable and well-satisfied, she set off across the moor towards the sea and Seagull Cottage.

Two hours later, she saw her first sign to Port Gawain and was soon travelling along the cliff-top road with a thrilling view of sparkling waves as far as the eye could see.

She swept down a steep hill and into the cove.

The tiny beach was dotted with holidaymakers and brightly coloured beach towels. Seagulls swooped and wheeled above them.

What few houses there were clung to the cliffs on either side of the tiny harbour. Opposite her road, another went round the harbour and up a hill and disappeared into the distance.

She turned into a tiny car park, switched off the engine and climbed out. The air was fresh and salty. She breathed deeply and smiled to herself. You never forgot the smell of Cornwall.

It was late afternoon but the sun was still hot. A cold drink would be a life saver, she decided, and looked around.

On one side of the small square was an old inn, the Lugger. Facing it, on the other side, a severe grey stone chapel. Opposite the car park, she was relieved to see a brightly painted cafe. Next door was the village shop which Caro had mentioned.

She crossed the square to the cafe.

A few sun-tanned holidaymakers sat chatting in the corner, but she imagined most people would be on the beach.

After ordering an orange juice, Jessica asked the small, plump owner if she knew Seagull Cottage. The woman's pleasant face broke into a smile.

'Course I do, my lover. Been 'ere all my life, I 'ave, so I reckon I know all the cottages.' She placed the tall glass of juice, tinkling temptingly with ice, on the counter. 'You 'ere on holiday?'

Jessica explained that she was holidaying with three friends and that she intended to stay on when they'd gone, to paint.

'You painting Seagull Cottage?' The woman began to polish the gleaming coffee machine, then stopped and laid her arms on the counter, prepared to chat. 'Very quaint, that is. 'Course it's been done up — prettified, if you know what I mean. Cottages never looked like that in the old days. But the visitors like it.'

Jessica finished her drink and the woman accompanied her to the door to offer her directions. 'Just go up the hill — fifty yards or so — and you'll come to it. White with blue shutters. You can't miss it.'

Jessica thanked her and, promising to return with her friends, crossed the square to the car park. She looked across at the other buildings as she unlocked the car. She wasn't sure about the church but she knew they'd visit the Lugger for some meals.

She drove slowly up the road and soon found Seagull Cottage. The windows were open and white net curtains fluttered in the sea breeze. Someone had arrived before her.

As she got out of the car, the front

door opened and Caro stood there, a welcoming smile on her face.

'Jessica! You made it! Come in. The others will be here soon. They're coming by train and taxi.'

The door opened straight into a cool living-room.

'This is wonderful,' sighed Jessica. 'I'm so hot.'

'How about a swim as soon as the others arrive?' suggested Caro.

She showed Jessica where to park her car then gave her a tour of the cottage. The ceilings were low, but pale cream painted walls made the most of the light which penetrated the tiny windows. Paintings of various sizes and subjects covered the walls of the little sitting-room and the side of the stairs.

There were touches of bright colour: a fat cream sofa piled with colourful cushions, red and green rugs covering the wooden floors, and polished mahogany tables bearing brightly patterned china.

'Isn't it cute?' Jessica enthused. 'So much in such a small space.' She leaned out of a tiny bedroom window. 'And right above the harbour. What a wonderful view!'

Voices from below sent them hurrying down the narrow, twisting wooden stairs. Kit and Anya had arrived.

'Swim?' Caro asked. 'We can eat later — unless you're hungry.'

'No. A swim,' they agreed.

'Just leave your bags here and we'll sort ourselves out when we get back,' said Caro.

★   ★   ★

Half an hour later they were all settling themselves on the minute beach at the side of the harbour. Kit stretched herself luxuriously on her colourful towel.

'How long have we got? Four days? I intend to enjoy every minute of them.'

'Don't get too settled there,' Caro warned. 'We've come to swim while it's still sunny.'

'Leave me alone.' Kit flapped a

dismissive hand at her. 'Swimming is too much like hard work. I intend to lie here and rest.'

Jessica jumped up. 'Well, I'm going in to swim. The water looks so inviting. Come on,' she called to the other two.

They ran down to the water and straight in with shrieks of surprise as the cold waves splashed up their hot bodies.

Anya wasn't much of a swimmer and chose to remain in the shallows near the beach but Jessica and Caro set out with firm strokes towards the deeper water.

'If the weather holds, we must come down every day,' Jessica shouted above the slap of the waves. 'This is wonderful.'

'I think we've come far enough, though,' Caro shouted back. 'We should go back now.'

'OK.'

They turned and began to swim back towards the shore, but suddenly Jessica gave a scream.

'Caro! My leg! Cramp! Oh — oh, the pain! Caro, help me!'

Caro looked back towards the beach. Anya was still swimming near the shore but Kit was looking their way. Caro waved her arms above her head and shouted, 'Help! Help!' with all the volume she could manage.

She grabbed Jessica and began to tow her towards the beach, but the other girl was struggling and Caro was afraid they would both go under.

Suddenly she was aware of another body powering through the water. Strong masculine arms reached across and gripped Jessica by the shoulders. With powerful strokes the stranger kicked out and supported the trembling girl until they reached the beach.

Kit and Anya ran towards him as he carried Jessica back to their towels as though she were as light as a child. He lowered her carefully and began to massage her leg as Kit draped a towel round her and Anya poured some hot coffee from a flask.

The stranger — he introduced himself as Chris — accepted a drink and smiled at Jessica.

'You'll be all right now,' he said. 'I think you were frightened more than anything else. But don't go back into the water today.'

'What a good thing you were here.' Jessica returned the smile shyly. 'I can't thank you enough.'

Kit was looking at the back of his strange swimming costume. '*Lifeguard*,' she read out. 'Really? I wouldn't have thought this beach was big enough for a lifeguard.'

'I'm based at St Ives,' he said. 'It's my day off so I'm visiting a few different beaches today.'

'Ready to save maidens in distress.' Caro laughed.

'Well, you never know,' he said. 'And the words give people confidence. They trust me, y'know?'

'Are you American?' Kit asked, her ear caught by his accent. 'You're certainly not English.'

'Yes. I'm over here for the summer.' He stood up in one sinuous movement.

'Well, if you ladies are all right now, I'll be off. Thanks for the coffee.' He put his hand to his forehead in a salute.

Jessica thanked him again and they watched as he set off across the beach with firm strides.

'Well,' said Anya, 'he can rescue me any time!'

'The sun's going in,' said Kit. 'Let's go back to the cottage.'

They collected their towels and bags and climbed the hill to Seagull Cottage. By the time they reached there, Jessica was feeling quite her old self and ready to laugh at what had happened.

'I wonder whether we'll see him again?' Anya mused.

'Perhaps he'll come looking for Jessica,' Caro suggested.

'He needn't bother,' Jessica protested.

'Oh, I forgot, you've got someone in mind, haven't you?' said Caro.

'No, I haven't! I don't want a man. I want to concentrate on my painting.'

They had reached the cottage and trooped inside.

'I'll put the kettle on for tea,' Caro said, 'then we'll decide on bedrooms. Cream tea on the patio in half an hour, so you'd better be quick if you want to unpack first.'

The tiny patio at the back of the cottage was just big enough for a table and chairs and a few plants in tubs. The cliff face formed the back wall and provided shade from the sun in the afternoon. But now the sun had almost gone in and the girls draped cardigans round their shoulders.

'Tuck in,' said Caro, passing round a plate of scones. 'Fresh today.'

She'd placed a bowl of clotted cream and another of strawberry jam on the table and her friends needed no more urging to help themselves.

Jessica looked around at her friends. 'This was a wonderful idea. We should have got together long ago.'

As they began to chat and reminisce, the years since they'd left the art school dropped away and they regained their easy friendship again. The air was full of, 'Do you remember . . . ' and 'What about when we . . . '

After a while, Jessica remembered that she had promised to phone Hilly.

'Of course,' said Caro, when she asked if she might use the telephone.

'I just want to phone my friend to say I've arrived safely but I forgot to recharge my mobile.'

'Don't tell him about the lifeguard,' Kit advised, and Jessica decided not to mention the incident in the sea that afternoon, either.

'It's not a he, it's a girlfriend — Hilly,' said Jessica. 'I won't be a moment.'

Hilly was pleased to hear from her.

'Ian's missing you already,' she said with a little giggle. 'He's here now. He came round to see if I'd heard from you.'

'Well, don't put him on,' Jessica warned. 'I don't want to use the phone for too long. Tell him I'll see him in a few days.'

She replaced the receiver and stood for a few minutes gazing out of the window at the boats bobbing at anchor below the window.

Missing me, she thought. I miss him, too. Wouldn't it be fun if he was here in Cornwall? So why didn't I want to speak to him? She turned away from the window. Perhaps I was afraid I might reveal my true feelings. It's so hard to pretend I'm happy with just friendship.

Anya came to find her. 'We've decided to go down to the Lugger for a meal at eight,' she said. 'Is that all right with you?'

'Fine. That'll give us time to unpack.'

They climbed the wooden stairs together. Jessica was sharing a bedroom with Caro.

'You can have the bed by the window,' Caro said as her friend came into the bedroom. 'If you sit up in bed in the morning, you can see the sea.'

Jessica changed into jeans and a loose white cotton smock and went downstairs to join the others.

'Good. Now we can go,' said Kit as Jessica appeared. 'I'm starving.'

'When were you anything else?' Anya

said with a laugh.

The sun had fully sunk behind the hill but the evening was light and refreshingly cool. The girls walked slowly down the hill and across the square to the old inn. It was crowded but they found a corner table and were soon ordering drinks and studying the menu. Now there was less chat and laughter between them. Travelling and the day's sunshine were having an effect upon them all and they felt drowsy.

'I hope you can stay awake long enough to eat your meals,' said Caro.

Food roused them a little. Kit studied a notice on the wall opposite their table: 'Come and dance the night away at the Lugger Inn,' she read. 'Tomorrow at eight. Shall we go? It could be fun.'

'I'm too tired,' groaned Anya.

'You won't be tired tomorrow after a good night's sleep,' said Kit. 'What d'you say?' She looked round the table. 'Shall we go?'

After a moment's thought, the others nodded.

Lying in her strange bed that night, Jessica took a while to fall asleep. She listened to the splash of water against the harbour wall beneath the cottage and the metallic clang of the ratlines and the anchor chains.

Caro, in the other bed, had fallen asleep straight away. The sounds of a harbour at night were not strange to her.

Jessica rolled on to her other side and closed her eyes. Unbidden, thoughts of Ian flashed into her mind. Was he thinking of her? Hilly had said he was missing her. Would she see him when she returned home? He'd said he just wanted friendship. Did that include travelling forty miles to see her occasionally?

She must try not to think of him, to concentrate on her painting. She opened her eyes for a few seconds but when she closed them again, his face was still there behind her eyes, in her mind. She blew a kiss into the darkness, rolled on to her back and slept.

* ★ ★

'Today we're going to do a grand tour of Cornwall,' Caro announced at breakfast. 'No swimming, no sunbathing.'

'Beaches and sunbathing tomorrow,' agreed Kit, jumping up and beginning to clear the table.

Half an hour later, they were all in the car and ready to set off.

Cornwall was crowded — it was the height of the tourist season — but Caro knew the secret ways through the countryside. They drove down quiet lanes with high banks on either side covered with clouds of white cow parsley.

'Where are we going first?' asked Anya.

'If they're not too crowded, I want to show you some of the little villages,' Caro said. 'But they're all tourist spots so we may not be able to park. We'll start with the artists' town, St Ives.'

'Where Chris is a lifeguard,' Kit remembered. 'Perhaps we'll bump into him.'

They parked in the car park at the

top of a hill and began the steep walk downwards through narrow, twisting cobbled streets to the front, until Caro turned into a doorway and led the way up steep steps to a cafe above. They found a table in the wide window overlooking the harbour.

'This is a wonderful vantage point,' said Jessica. 'I should think everyone who visits St Ives strolls along here at some time in the day.'

They people-watched until finally Caro said, 'Come on, drink up. We must be on our way.'

The climb up to the car park, past artists' studios, shady courtyards and cottage walls covered with climbing shrubs, was a source of delight, but they were soon on their way again . . .

Lying in bed that night, Jessica thought back over a most delightful day, her memories a jumble of impressions: little coves with white sand and sparkling turquoise water; a stroll along the coastal path past old engine houses, relics of the tin-mining industry, now romantically covered with trailing ivy; a view across the water to St Michael's Mount, crowned with its white castle whose turrets gleamed in the sunshine.

'There's a cobbled causeway under the water,' Caro had informed them. 'You can walk across at low tide.'

A delicious lunch of crab sandwiches and, later, a scrumptious tea of warm scones, strawberry jam and clotted cream had rounded the day off.

Jessica rolled on to her back. There was so much to remember. She thought of the little villages. Mousehole was her favourite and she intended to return there when she could.

They'd arrived back at the cottage in the early evening, clutching pebbles, shells and souvenirs. Jessica had bought a bracelet of beautifully polished tiny pebbles for Hilly. She'd wondered whether to look for a gift for Ian, but decided that a small tin of Cornish fairings might seem less personal.

'Tea on the patio again?' Caro had suggested. 'But no cream tea, we're going out dancing later, remember?'

'Oh yes, the dance at the Lugger,' Anya had chimed in. 'Have we all brought evening gowns?'

'I daresay we can find something suitable for the Lugger,' Kit had said with a yawn. 'Though I don't know that I've got enough energy left to dance.'

'It was your suggestion,' Caro had reminded her. 'You were very enthusiastic last night.'

Kit had grinned, stretched out in her armchair like a cat and closed her eyes. 'Give me fifteen minutes and I'll be ready to go . . .'

Lying wakeful, Jessica let her mind wander back over the girls' preparation for their evening out and the dance itself . . .

She chose to wear a long rose-pink cotton skirt and a deep pink tee-shirt with a rope of pearl beads twisted about her neck, and her hair had been brushed until it shone.

When she looked at the effect in the mirror she was quite pleased with her appearance and found herself musing, What if I was dressing up for Ian? If we were off to the dance together?

Caro came into the room. 'You look quite beautiful,' she said. 'Now let me have the mirror, please, if you've finished.'

When they'd eaten their meal at the Lugger Inn, they were directed into the back, where they settled themselves round a table at the side of the already crowded room. The centre of the floor had been cleared for dancing.

They sat out the first two dances.

'D'you think we'll get any partners?' Anya wondered aloud. 'We don't know anyone and most girls seem to have brought partners.'

'Now everyone on the floor. You don't need partners,' the MC's voice commanded. 'Two circles: ladies inside, gentlemen outside. You walk round and when the music stops, you dance with the person opposite you.'

'Come on.' Kit jumped to her feet. 'This is our chance.'

They joined the circle in the centre

115

and were soon moving round the room. The music stopped and Jessica found herself opposite a small, rather square man who grabbed her unceremoniously and began to jig about. Although he was perfectly nice, she was glad when the dance ended.

They were off again in their circle and this time her partner was tall and thin. He was a good dancer but kept smiling across the room at a plump, fair girl, obviously his real partner.

Just as Jessica was beginning to wonder whether she really liked this form of dancing, the MC stepped forward again.

'Now it's a competition,' he said. 'The best pair of dancers will win a prize. Remember, you must dance with the person you stop opposite.'

Jessica joined her circle again. Two circuits of the floor and the music stopped.

'Goodness!' she exclaimed to the man opposite. 'You!' It was the lifeguard, Chris.

'I hoped you might be here.' He held out a hand and slipped it round her waist.

'I didn't see you in the men's circle when they went round before,' she said.

'I've just arrived.' He smiled down at her with bright hazel eyes. 'We seem to be doing well together. Let's try for the prize.'

Jessica had always loved dancing, and although Gregory had been willing to take the floor with her, he'd had two left feet. Now she knew she had found a partner with whom she could really dance.

Together they twirled and glided till some couples moved to the side to give them more room. Ignoring the crowd, Jessica abandoned herself to the music and the movement and the sensation of being held in Chris's arms.

It was no contest. Before the MC could announce the winners, the room had burst into spontaneous applause for Jessica and Chris. Flushed with triumph and excitement, Jessica caught the eyes of her friends. Like everyone else they were smiling and applauding loudly.

'You two were just like Fred Astaire and Ginger Rogers,' Caro laughed when they joined them.

'Let me get some drinks,' Chris said when he'd greeted them. 'You must all be thirsty.'

'I'll come and help you carry them.' Anya was quickly on her feet.

'I knew he'd be here looking for you,' Kit said.

'He couldn't have known we'd be here,' Jessica retorted.

'It was an easy guess. Most holiday-makers would come to a dance.'

'What have you won?' asked Caro.

Chris and Anya had returned with the drinks and he heard the question. 'A meal for two. At the Lugger, of course.' He looked at Jessica.

'Very nice,' said Kit. 'When shall you go?'

'We'll all go,' said Jessica firmly. 'Tomorrow night.'

A flicker of disappointment crossed Chris's face, but he said cheerfully, 'Good idea. I'll call for you at eight.'

For the rest of the evening, Chris danced with each of the girls in turn, ending up with Jessica. The dance was slow, and he held her close.

'Didn't you want to have dinner with me on your own?' he asked.

Jessica studied his sunburnt face. He was very attractive, but she wasn't looking for romance — although there was no reason why she shouldn't enjoy herself. Gregory didn't want her. And Ian didn't want to be serious; he probably went out with other girls. The thought disturbed her and she concentrated on Chris.

'Let's just enjoy tomorrow as a group,' she said lightly.

They danced in silence for a while then he said, 'I'm heading back to the States at the weekend. That's why I wanted to have dinner just with you. Give me something to think about on my flight home.'

'But we'll probably never meet again,' she protested.

'Why not? People fly backwards and

forwards across the Atlantic all the time. It's no big deal.'

As the music ended, they walked slowly back to the others.

'We're going now,' Jessica said. 'I'll see you tomorrow.'

'I'll call for you at eight.' Chris looked round the group, gave them a smile and a salute and vanished through the crowd of dancers.

Jessica was quiet as they strolled back to the cottage. Now she had even more to think about.

'What Would Ian Think?'

The telephone rang as they were about to leave the cottage the next morning for the beach. The call was for Caro so she sent her friends on ahead. 'I'll join you in a moment,' she said. 'Go and bag a good spot on the sand.'

When she joined them she said nothing about the call.

'Now for a spot of serious sun-bathing,' she said as she spread out her beach towel and took sun-cream from her bag. 'I know it's bad for you, but vitamin D is good and the sun provides vitamin D, so I'm going to bake for a while.'

'When we're back at work we'll think of this,' said Anya, 'and wish we were here.'

Kit said nothing, just lay back and closed her eyes.

Jessica sat up and gazed at the waves.

What should she do about Chris? What would Ian think if he knew about her dinner date with another man? But what right did he have to think anything of it? He didn't want any kind of commitment between them.

With a sigh she lay down on her towel and lifted her face to the sun.

'Anything wrong?' Anya asked.

'No. Just complicated thoughts. They'll sort themselves out.'

After a while, they all went for a cooling swim, and then as the time approached midday, Caro suggested returning to the cottage for lunch.

'We shouldn't sunbathe for the next few hours,' she said, gathering up her towel and beach bag. 'It's the hottest part of the day.'

The others agreed and they made their way up the little hill to the cottage.

'Cheese toasties?' Caro suggested. 'They won't take long to make.'

They were soon sitting around the table on the patio with cheese toasties, orange juice and a bowl of fruit to share.

'Delicious!' Kit wiped her mouth with a napkin. 'I could get used to this life.'

They sat in comfortable silence for a while, then, as so often happened between these four old friends, began to reminisce.

'Remember the fancy dress party when we all went in Kit's car wearing our costumes and the car broke down?' said Anya.

'And we had to walk the last half mile,' Kit chimed in.

'Jessica was a duck with bright yellow legs,' Anya spluttered. 'We all sewed the paper feathers on to her costume.'

Jessica joined in the laughter. 'I felt a real fool walking along the street as a duck.'

'What about when we nearly burnt down the college,' said Caro.

'Oh yes,' Jessica remembered. 'We'd made a papier mache dragon and put it on a board to dry.'

'And we decided to put it down in the boiler room where it was warmer, and it caught fire,' laughed Kit. 'If the caretaker hadn't found it in time we really would have burnt down the whole building.'

'Imagine the headlines in the local paper,' Caro finished, wiping her eyes.

'We had some fun, didn't we?' said Kit. The others nodded, thinking back.

'It would be nice to go somewhere different tonight,' said Anya after a while.

'Well, we can't. Our prize was a voucher for the Lugger,' Jessica pointed out.

'Why didn't you agree to go with Chris on your own?' asked Caro. 'You do like him, don't you?'

'Perhaps she's thinking of her mystery man back home?' said Anya.

'We came for a holiday together,' said Jessica. 'It didn't seem right to go off with someone on my own. All for one and one for all. Remember?'

'So you weren't thinking of — what was his name? — Ian, wasn't it?'

'Yes, Ian,' said Jessica. 'No, I wasn't thinking of him, as I'm sure he wasn't thinking of me. We're just friends.'

'But you do like Chris,' Caro persisted.

Jessica tipped back her head and looked up at the vivid blue sky above them, contemplating.

'Yes, I do like him,' she said after a while. 'But he's going back to America in a few days. I don't expect to see him again.'

'Stranger things have happened,' said Kit. 'Perhaps he'll return one day and claim you.'

Jessica threw a napkin at her. 'Don't be ridiculous! Let's change the subject.'

'The phone call I had as we went out — ' Caro looked around at the group. 'Some friends of my parents who live just along the coast are having a barbecue this evening. We're invited. I accepted for three of us.' She looked at Jessica. 'I thought you might prefer to go out with Chris.'

All eyes turned towards Jessica who flushed.

'Well — I — '

'That's settled then,' said Anya. 'I'm sure Chris will be relieved.'

Caro, Anya and Kit left before Chris arrived at the cottage. Jessica watched them go from the window. She wasn't sure whether she was sad not to be going to the barbecue with them or glad to have Chris to herself.

There was no doubting Chris's feelings when he arrived and discovered that he and Jessica were to go out alone.

'Your friends are great fun,' he said, 'but I have to admit that I wanted the evening to be for the two of us alone.'

Looking at him, Jessica decided that it was what she wanted, too.

The inn pulled out all the stops for their prize dinner. They were given the best seats, champagne and a delicious meal.

'Tell me about your family,' said Jessica as they settled down to coffee and chocolates.

'There's not much to tell. There's just Dad and my sister Mary-Lou. My mother died when I was born. What about you?'

'Parents, and I have a sister, too — Claire. She's in Canada. And is there a girlfriend waiting for you back home?'

Chris smiled. 'No. Not now. There was one. We finished before I came to England. You?'

'Not really,' she said vaguely. She felt she couldn't discuss Gregory.

'I find that hard to believe,' he said.

'Well, there might be someone. We haven't known each other long.'

'He'd better make up his mind quickly. A girl like you will soon be snapped up.' He took a chocolate from the dish on the table and gazed at it thoughtfully before popping it into his mouth. 'Would you write to me? Could we exchange addresses?'

After a moment's thought, Jessica shook her head. 'I don't think so,' she said gently. 'Let's leave this as a very pleasant but brief holiday friendship.'

He put an elbow on the table and his chin in his hand and studied her.

'Shame. Are you quite sure?'

'I'm sure. I have a few complications in my life at the moment,' Jessica answered. 'I really don't want any more. I've decided to devote myself to my career from now on.'

Chris nodded slowly. 'Fair enough. A holiday friendship it will be.' He sat forward and poured them each another coffee. 'So, tell me about this career. What do you do exactly?'

★ ★ ★

Later, as they walked slowly back to the cottage hand in hand, Jessica thought it had been one of the most gentle and enjoyable evenings of her life. Chris was friendly, even affectionate, but not demanding. In his company, she felt herself relax. There were no pressures, no decisions to be made.

They reached the cottage.

'It seems too nice to go in,' said Chris, looking up at the starlit sky.

The windows of the cottage were lit

up. Jessica's friends were back. She'd better join them.

'You could come in for a drink if you like,' she offered.

'Thanks, but no. I have a lot of sorting out to do if I'm to be on that plane at the weekend. It's amazing how much junk you acquire in even a few months.'

They stood facing each other. Jessica held out a hand. 'Goodbye, Chris, and good luck. Thank you again for saving my life.'

He took her hand in both of his. 'Goodbye, Jessica. I don't suppose I could have just one kiss?'

Jessica looked up at him. He really was very sweet.

'Just one,' she agreed.

He put his arms round her. His kiss was firm but brief. His voice was husky. 'Goodbye, Jessica, and the very best of luck to you.' He gave her a smile, turned, and was gone, walking briskly down the hill as he had walked across the sand when she had first met him.

She watched until he turned the corner at the bottom of the hill, then reached into her pocket for the door key. But then she paused . . .

The moon was bright above her and the night was warm. She wasn't ready to go in and face the teasing and the questions of her friends. The gentle mood of the evening would be broken.

Instead she walked slowly back across the road, leaned on the wall and looked over at the harbour below.

The boats rocked gently at anchor. Her artist's eye took in the details of the scene to recall when she was far away from Cornwall.

Slow footsteps approaching made her turn quickly. A tall man was coming towards her. A tall man she recognised.

'I thought you were off men? It didn't look like it from where I was standing.' His voice was bitter, totally unlike him.

'Ian! What are you doing here? Are you following me?'

'I thought you were staying with girlfriends?'

'So you're spying on me? How dare you!'

'I thought you were staying with a group of girlfriends,' he repeated.

'I am — not that it's any of your business. My friends are in the cottage over there.'

'So who was the guy? You seemed very friendly.'

'That's right — friendly! Oh, and he saved me from drowning.'

'He what? What happened?' He took a step towards her and put his hands on her shoulders. 'Tell me.'

'I got cramp. He's a lifeguard. He saved me.'

Silently he put his arms round her and held her close. 'I'm sorry, but when I saw him kiss you . . . '

'A kiss goodbye,' she said. 'He's going back to America at the weekend. We didn't exchange addresses and I shan't see him again.' She pulled herself free of his embrace. 'Anyway, what has it to do with you? You said no commitment. Just friendship. So I can be friends with other people, too.'

He leaned on the wall beside her and gazed down at the boats below.

'I'm sorry,' he said. 'You're right. I have no business questioning you. But I missed you. So I begged Hilly for your address and followed you. And when I saw you with another man — well, I just flipped.'

'Where are you staying?' she asked after a pause.

'At the Lugger Inn.'

'But that's where we've just had dinner.'

'I know. I saw you as I passed the dining-room door. 'I'd hoped to surprise you, but when I saw — well, it didn't seem a good idea.'

'We won the meal in a dance competition,' she explained. 'I was there with my friends. Chris turned up and we danced together. And we won the prize — a meal at the inn.'

'What about your friends?'

'They went to a barbecue. But they're back at the cottage now. I was just going in.'

He turned and stood with his back against the wall looking down at her. 'Are you going home tomorrow?'

'They are. I'm staying on for two or three days to work on the cottage painting.'

He was silent for a few minutes, thinking. Then he said, 'Would you mind if I stayed in the village for two days?'

'Shouldn't you be at work?'

He smiled. 'I'm allowed a few days off if I want them. I'll work extra hard when I go back.'

'I shan't be able to go about with you,' she warned. 'I'll have to work hard to do all I need in two days.'

'But not in the evenings,' he protested. 'You can see me for dinner.'

I won't seem too keen, Jessica told herself. He can't expect me to come running every time he crooks his finger. But secretly she was delighted with his suggestion. She looked up at him.

'Just for dinner,' she agreed. 'But I must have the days to myself. Now I'd better go in. My friends will be wondering what's happened to me.'

Ian watched her cross the road and reach up to unlock the cottage door. The sound of laughter reached him as the door opened.

He remained leaning against the harbour wall, watching the cottage, for ten minutes. His feelings as he saw Jessica being kissed by another man had startled him. He'd known he was attracted to her, and had already decided that when she said she had definitely finished with Gregory, he would stake his claim. But now he recognised his feelings as acute jealousy. And that could mean only one thing: he was in love with Jessica, and he couldn't wait to make her fall in love with him, however much she protested that she'd finished with men and romance.

But what if she'd fallen for the lifeguard? She might even have contemplated going to America. Then he really would have lost her.

He pushed himself away from the

wall. It was a good thing he'd decided to follow her to Cornwall.

For the next two days he would shadow her closely. There would be no more encounters with strange men!

If only he could be sure she'd never go back to Gregory. Well, time would tell.

* * *

After a noisy breakfast next morning, the girls left for their respective journeys home.

Jessica had been teased about Chris and scolded for not bringing him back to say goodbye.

'But no, you kept him to yourself till the last minute,' Kit teased.

'When are you going to America?' Anya wanted to know.

In vain Jessica protested that they had said goodbye for good and would not be in touch. She was thankful that they had not seen Ian last night or she would have had no peace from them.

At last they were gone. Jessica, waving from the doorstep, gazed down at the little beach beyond the harbour and the rocks opposite the cottage. That would be the perfect place to sit and make the first sketch.

She collected her sketching equipment and a small folding stool and set off down the hill to the harbour, stopping on the way at the little shop to buy two bottles of mineral water. It was a warm day.

She positioned her stool on a wide slab of rock almost directly opposite the cottage. For some time she studied the little house, then picked up a pencil and made a rapid sketch indicating the shape of the building, the roof, the doors and the windows. Then, using her special code, she indicated the shades and colours she would use.

The sun was high in the sky. It was getting very hot. Jessica adjusted the large towel she had draped over her shoulders for protection, and reached for a bottle of water. As she unscrewed it, she glanced down towards the harbour. A man was walking purposefully in her direction. She watched his approach.

'Found you,' said Ian with satisfaction.

'It couldn't have been difficult,' she said dismissively. 'You knew I was painting Seagull Cottage, so it was a fair guess I'd be sitting opposite it.'

'Don't deride my efforts.'

Ian selected another flat rock nearby and lowered himself gingerly on to it. 'Ouch! This is hot!'

Jessica smiled. 'You should have brought something to sit on if you're so delicate.'

He studied her. 'Why so prickly? Am I in the way?'

'I am rather busy. Hadn't you noticed?' she said as she screwed the top back on to the bottle and placed it in the shade.

He glanced at her easel. 'It's very good,' he commented. 'But you haven't got very far, have you?'

'I've done a terrific amount of work,' she said indignantly. 'Proper preparation is very important. Anyway, what do you know about painting?'

He held up his hands in a gesture of peace. 'Nothing,' he agreed. 'I'm sorry, I'm sure it's almost finished.'

She sighed impatiently. 'It's not nearly finished — and it won't be if you keep interrupting me.' So saying, she picked up a pencil.

'Wait. Put that pencil down. It's one o'clock.'

'So what?' Shading her eyes, she looked across at Seagull Cottage and prepared to get back to work.

'It's lunchtime.'

'I told you, I'm busy. I haven't time to go looking for lunch.'

Ian held up a large cooler bag. 'No need. It's here.'

She put down the pencil again. 'You mean you've — '

'I've brought lunch for both of us. Hot pasties, what else? That's why I put them in the cooler bag. Keeps them warm. Don't tell me you can't stop long enough to eat a pasty?'

'But my hands are all painty.'

'You could do what the old miners did and hold it by the thick handles at each end. That's why they were designed that way.'

'You think of everything, don't you?' she said with a grin. 'What would I do without you? No, don't answer that,' she said hastily as he opened his mouth to reply.

They sat and ate their pasties with enjoyment. Below, the beach was beginning to fill up with holidaymakers.

'Shall we have a swim later on?' Ian inquired.

Jessica wiped the crumbs from her fingers.

'That would be nice. I'm so hot. But I can't stop right now. I really need to get on with this.'

Ian stood up. 'I'll go back to the inn. I have some phone calls to make in any case. When do you think you'll be ready to leave?'

Jessica consulted her watch. 'Give me three hours,' she said. 'I'll have had enough sun by then.'

'Three hours,' he agreed. 'See you then.'

She watched him walk away then turn and give her a wave. She waved back and picked up a pencil, but when she appraised the scene, she found that the sun had moved during her break and she was now in the shadow of the cliff. It would be more comfortable to work.

Wasn't that typical of Ian, she thought. He had known she wouldn't want to bother with lunch so he had brought it to her. A little smile played around her lips as she worked away. She'd wished he was in Cornwall with her, and now he was. So wishes could come true.

★　★　★

At five o'clock he was back again.

'Come on. You've done enough for

today, and the water looks very inviting.'

Stretching, Jessica agreed. She gathered up her belongings while Ian took her stool and easel, then they clambered over the rocks and down to the harbour only to climb slowly back up the hill to the cottage. Ian looked around with interest as they entered.

'Tiny, but perfect,' he commented. 'I could imagine living here if I was an old salt.'

'Old salts lived here with their wives and several children,' she said. 'The cottage might be tiny but it was home to quite large families.'

Jessica went upstairs for her swimsuit and towel, made a flask of coffee, and they set off for the beach.

'Is this where you nearly drowned?' Ian asked as they spread their towels and rubbed suncream into their arms.

'Yes. I was swimming with Caro. We went out a bit too far and I got cramp.'

'And were rescued by your handsome lifeguard.'

'Don't mock! If Chris hadn't been there I might have drowned. Caro did her best but she couldn't manage on her own.'

'I'm sorry. I shall be eternally grateful to him. Here, let me rub some cream into your back.'

Jessica turned and leaned forward so that he could massage the suncream on to her shoulders and back. She sat quite still as his fingers caressed her skin, willing him not to stop.

'One thing puzzles me,' Ian said behind her. 'How does such a tiny beach come to have a lifeguard?'

'It doesn't. He was based at St Ives and just happened to be visiting here during some time off.' She stood up. 'That's enough about Chris. Race you to the water!'

* * *

'You've caught the sun today.' Ian looked across the table at Jessica's flushed face. 'It suits you.' He had booked them a table for dinner at one of the local inns.

Jessica touched the back of her hand to her cheek and felt the warmth. 'What will I look like after another day on the cliffs tomorrow? But I must sit out there. I need to do as much of the cottage as I can. I'll be going home the day after.'

Ian handed her a menu. 'How's your appetite after a day in the fresh air? They specialize in seafood, of course. D'you fancy deep fried squid with chilli mayonnaise?'

She looked at him with an expression of alarm.

'Squid? I don't think so!' She studied the menu. 'Sea bass with basil and mushrooms sounds better.'

'And I'll have sea bream with herbs, tomatoes and olives.'

Jessica looked around the old inn with its darkwood tables and country-style chairs. The stone walls were painted white and hung with pictures of sailing ships and pirates.

'This place looks very old,' she said. 'Do you think it's authentic?'

'I believe it is. A notice on the wall by the fireplace says it has a secret tunnel and two ghosts.'

'Perhaps it was a smugglers' inn and the tunnel goes down to a cave on the beach.'

'What about the ghosts?'

She thought for a moment. 'Maybe one was a smuggler and the other a customs officer and they killed each other in the secret tunnel.'

'What an imagination!' he said admiringly. 'You should write a novel.'

'Good idea. And I could illustrate it, too.'

The food, when it came, was excellent, and they ate in silence for a while, savouring every mouthful. Then Jessica said, 'You can stay another day, can't you?'

'I didn't want to tell you now and spoil the evening but — no. I have to return tomorrow.'

Her face fell. 'Business, I suppose?'

'Yes. A good account. The MD will be in Breverton for just one day, and I need to see him.'

'So you're going back?'

'Tomorrow morning. I'm sorry, Jessica. I was really looking forward to spending another day with you.'

Jessica sighed and picked up her knife and fork again.

'It can't be helped. Maybe I'll do more work if I don't stop to go swimming with you!'

'I don't like to think of you here on your own.'

She shrugged carelessly. 'Don't worry about it. It's what I'd planned in the first place. I shall be fine. It's only for one day and one night.'

'Have you heard from your friends? Did they get home all right?'

'Mm. They all phoned when I was getting ready to come out this evening. They envy me — still being here, I mean.'

'What are you going to do about Aunt Ramona's proposal that you should go out to Italy and paint the villa?'

'What would you do? She seems rather fearsome. Yet I'd be there with her for a week.'

'But not alone. Hilly would be with you, wouldn't she?'

Jessica shrugged. 'Probably. But we haven't discussed it. I'm waiting till I see her again.'

Ian smiled. 'Don't be afraid of Aunt Ramona. She can't help being — what did you say — fearsome?'

'*You're* afraid of her.'

Ian began to laugh. 'Yes, but I'm her nephew. She can say what she likes to me.'

The waiter appeared and unobtrusively took their plates.

'Can I bring you anything else?' he asked. 'The dessert menu, perhaps?'

Ian raised an eyebrow at Jessica. 'Pudding, or just coffee?'

'Just coffee for me, please.'

★ ★ ★

Their coffees were served in the lounge, to a discreet corner sofa near the fireplace. Jessica studied the arrangement of grasses in a wide brass bowl set in the centre of the empty hearth.

'I expect they have a big log fire here in winter,' she said dreamily. 'It must look very cosy.'

Ian studied her profile. 'Shall we come back one day and find out?' he asked.

She felt herself flush under her suntan. 'We'll probably be much too busy.' She sipped her coffee in some confusion.

'Will you come to the Lugger and have breakfast with me before I leave in the morning?' he asked, changing the subject.

'That would be nice. What time?'

'Oh, about nine. I don't have to leave particularly early.'

Jessica felt a glow of happiness. Now she wouldn't have to say goodbye this evening.

'Would you like a nightcap?' he asked presently.

'I shan't need anything to make me

sleep,' she answered. 'Fresh air does just as well.'

He stood up and held out a hand to help her to her feet, then stooped slightly to drop a gentle kiss on her forehead.

'Dear Jessica,' he whispered.

She gazed up into his eyes. 'I'm so glad you came down.'

He was still holding her hand, and rubbed his thumb across her fingers. 'So am I.'

They strolled back to the cottage, his arm around her waist. As they reached the door, a fine misty rain began to fall.

'Do you want to come in until it stops?' she asked.

'It won't stop,' he said cheerfully. 'This kind of rain can go on for hours. But it'll probably be gone by the morning so you'll be able to do your painting.'

Jessica wondered whether he would kiss her again, and if he did, what it would mean. But he simply took the key from her hand and fitted it into the lock.

'In you go,' he said as he opened the

door. 'See you tomorrow about nine. Sweet dreams. Think of me as I do a one-minute-mile back down the hill before I get soaked,' he said, laughing ruefully.

Jessica locked the door behind him and sank into an armchair. But before she could have the luxury of thinking back over the evening, her mobile phone began to ring.

Hilly, she thought, or maybe Caro. She pulled it out of her handbag and pressed a button.

'Darling, where have you been? I've been ringing all evening.'

Mother! What now? She wasn't prepared to enter an argument about Gregory at eleven o'clock at night.

'Hello, Mother. Lovely to hear you. I'm sorry to miss your calls. I went out to dinner and switched off my phone.'

'I thought your friends had gone home?'

Her voice was accusing, as if she wanted to know who Jessica could possibly be with. But she asked no more questions. She sounded excited, as if she had some news of her own. Puzzled, Jessica waited.

'Darling, guess what? You know how your father's always doing competitions? Well, he's won a fantastic prize! He's always said someone has to win so why not him — and now it's actually happened.'

'Great! What's the prize?'

'A Mediterranean cruise for two! How about that?'

'That's wonderful. When do you go?'

'Next weekend. There's no reason to wait.'

'Quite right, too! Tell him congratulations from me.'

'You'll be home soon, won't you?' Mrs Lawrence asked. 'You can tell him yourself.'

'Well, actually I may be going away myself. To Italy. Hilly's mother has a villa there. She wants me to travel back with her quite soon — she's over here at the moment — and paint her villa on the lake.'

'Well!' Her mother was clearly impressed.

'So I don't know when I'll see you,' Jessica hurried on. 'If I'm not back before you leave, have a wonderful time.'

'We will. I'll be busy all week buying some new clothes. What a shame you won't be here to help me.'

'Take Auntie Vi with you. She's got good taste and she's been on a cruise. She'd be more help than me.'

'Good idea. Well, dear, I hope we see you before we leave. If not, we'll take loads of photographs to show you when we get back.'

Jessica switched off her phone. It seemed she'd subconsciously made up her mind.

'I'm going to Italy,' she had said. Good. So that was settled. And there would be no discussion about Gregory.

'I'm Going Away...'

Jessica decided to load her car with all she would need for the day, and drive down to the Lugger Inn the next morning. She'd attempted to carry everything and walk down, but with an easel under one arm, a canvas under the other and a bag on her back, she felt like a packhorse. Hardly the picture she wanted Ian to take with him on his journey home!

The evening rain had gone and it was a beautiful bright morning. Ian was walking up and down outside the inn as she pulled up.

'Am I late?' she called.

'No. I just felt like some fresh sea air before I return to the stale town air.' He held open the door for her to slide out. 'Breakfast will be ready when we want it. Shall we take a stroll round the harbour first?'

He took her arm and they set off towards the boats. The sun made little diamond flashes of light on the waves.

'I shall think of this scene all the way home,' he said.

'What a shame you can't stay one more day. I'll feel greedy having an extra day on my own.'

He took her hand and squeezed it. 'Lucky you! But some of us have to work.'

'I'll be working,' she said indignantly. 'This isn't a holiday. But I'm lucky to have a wonderful job that I can do in a lovely place like this.'

'And what about Aunt Ramona's villa? That's a beautiful place. Have you decided to go?'

'I haven't quite decided,' she fibbed, 'though it could lead to other commissions. I wonder when she'll be returning to Italy?'

'Next week, I believe.'

'Next week? Goodness, that doesn't give me much time.'

They walked on for a bit until Ian

glanced at his watch.

'Perhaps we should go back for breakfast now.'

Their short walk had given them both an appetite, and when they finished their bacon and eggs, Ian ordered more toast. Jessica was pleased; it meant they would have more time together.

'I have a long journey ahead of me,' said Ian, 'and you need to eat plenty so that you won't worry about lunch,' he said, pouring more coffee.

'I'll have no one to get it for me today,' she said, smiling at him.

All too soon they were finished and Jessica found herself outside again and waiting while he loaded bags into his car.

'That's everything,' he said. He put his arms round her and gave her a hug. 'Goodbye, Jessica. Thank you for your company at breakfast. Enjoy your last day.' He bent and kissed her forehead. Then he was in the car and driving out of the car park. A wave, and he was gone.

Jessica's eyes filled with tears, whether of disappointment or frustration, she wasn't sure. One tiny kiss on the forehead! Why couldn't he see that she had wanted him to take her in his arms and . . .

Friends, she reminded herself. We're just good friends. But why, then, had he come all this way to see her? And what about his jealous reaction to Chris? She sighed, lifted her painting equipment out of the car boot, and toted it carefully over to the rocks opposite Seagull Cottage.

She was soon lost in the task of capturing the little cottage on canvas. The painted white curtains fluttering out of a downstairs window set off the soft blue shutters. The front door was also blue and a hanging basket of scarlet geraniums gleamed against the ice cream white of the walls.

She added a faint plume of smoke curling out of a chimney pot where there was none. Artistic licence, she told herself.

Putting the brushes into a pot at her

feet, she took a miniature camera from her bag. Ian had taken several photographs of the cottage yesterday but she was a perfectionist and needed a few more. No good wondering about this feature or that when she was trying to finish the painting at home.

By now it was early afternoon and she was beginning to feel tired. She stood up, stretched and yawned. It had been a good day's work.

As she looked down at the boats, a little brown dog jumped from one to another and disappeared down a hatch. A sailor gathered up a tangle of nets and another swept his deck.

'I wonder where Ian is now?' she thought.

As if in answer to her musings, her phone rang.

'Jessica.' It was Ian. She felt her heart leap. 'Are you all right?'

'Fine. I'm just packing up. Where are you?'

'Snatching a quick coffee. I just wanted to hear your voice.'

She felt a catch in her throat. 'It

— it's lovely to hear you, too.'

'Must go. I'll see you soon. Bye, Jessica. Take care.'

He was gone. Slowly she closed the phone. He was thinking of her. That helped.

She concentrated on sorting out and packing up her paints and brushes in order not to leave anything behind.

At last she was ready and made her way over the rocks to the harbour and from there across the square to her car, thoughtful and reflective. Suddenly, though, it occurred to her that the pain in her stomach might not be romantic pangs of love but plain old hunger! She had eaten nothing since breakfast.

'Hello, my lover.' The woman behind the cafe counter recognised her from before and was happy to have company. 'What can I get you?'

'A Cornish cream tea, please,' said Jessica. 'I'm going home tomorrow, so this is my last chance to have one.'

'And I make a good one, though I say it myself.' The woman was busy filling a little teapot with water and placing crockery on a tray. 'Fresh today, these are.' She added two scones in a wicker basket. A dish of jam and another of clotted cream completed the tea. Jessica felt her mouth water and couldn't wait to begin.

'You're painting Seagull Cottage, aren't you? Is it finished?' the woman asked as she worked.

'Nearly. I'll finish it at home.'

'Lots of people come down here to paint,' said the woman. 'Supposed to be a special light.' She wiped the already spotless counter. 'Your friends gone home, then?'

'Oh, yes,' said Jessica. 'Yesterday.' She was finding it difficult to eat and answer the woman at the same time, and was glad when a party of visitors came into the cafe to lure her away.

* * *

She spent the evening packing her bags and tidying the cottage. Supper was a simple meal of scrambled eggs and some fruit. She couldn't face the inn on her own. There would be too many mcmorics.

At ten o'clock, her chores finished, she strolled across the road and looked down at the boats in the harbour below, thoughts of how her life had changed in the last few months crowding her mind.

By now, she should have been making final preparations for her wedding. Instead, she was heart-free and looking forward to developing her career. She was in Cornwall and soon she would be in Italy.

Heart-free? Was that true? Certainly Gregory no longer had a place in her heart. But what about Ian? Unseeing, she turned to look out at the darkened sea. Perhaps she had met Ian too soon after breaking up with Gregory and he was just a rebound attraction. Would she have fallen in love with him if she had met him before Gregory?

Yes! She had no doubts. She was in love with Ian in a way she had never loved Gregory. But what was the use? If they stayed friends for long enough, perhaps his feelings of friendship would turn to love. But could she wait around for that?

No, friendship was all there could be between them. She must settle for that or never see him again.

She returned to the cottage and locked the door against the cooling night air. As she ascended the stairs to her bedroom, her phone rang.

Ian! She sat on a stair to answer it.

'Jessica? Jessica? It's Gregory. How are you?'

'Gregory, it's past ten o'clock. What on earth do you want? I'm on my way to bed.'

'I met your friend Kay. She said you were in Cornwall. I wondered when you're coming back.'

'What does it have to do with you?'

'I want us to meet. We need to talk.'

'Do you think so?' Her voice was determined. 'I thought we said all there was to say last time we met.'

'And I suppose you haven't spoken to your mother yet.' His voice sounded bitter. 'I think I'll have to tell mine.'

'No. Not yet. My parents are going on a cruise very soon and I don't want to spoil it for them. I won't see them for a few weeks.'

'That suits you, doesn't it? You know what your mother will say.'

'Goodbye, Gregory. I have to go now.'

'What are you doing in Cornwall? Is that the furthest away you could get from me?' He sounded peevish.

'Goodbye, Gregory.' She switched off.

What was all that about? Was Gregory having second thoughts about breaking off their engagement?

She continued up the stairs, quite sure now that she wanted nothing more to do with her ex-fiancé.

★　★　★

Her journey back was uneventful except for another phone call. This time it was from Hilly.

161

'Jessica, I'm sorry but Mrs Carless, your guesthouse landlady, has gone into hospital. Would you mind staying with me for a week or two?'

'Hospital? Is it serious?'

'We don't know yet. She collapsed and they're keeping her in for tests.'

'Well — I could go straight home to my flat,' said Jessica.

'Please don't. Please come to me. I've missed your company while you've been away. And you know you can paint here perfectly well.'

With a little more persuasion, Jessica agreed. After all, Ramona Penn had wondered why she wasn't staying with Hilly. It seemed the natural thing to do.

Three days later, Ramona Penn again swept into the house and installed herself on a couch in the drawing-room.

'Well, young lady,' she addressed Jessica, 'have you come to a decision about my villa?'

'Yes,' Jessica said. 'I'd like to accept the commission. It sounds interesting and — different.'

Mrs Penn beamed. 'Wonderful. We leave on Saturday. Hilly is coming with us.'

'Saturday?' Jessica faltered. 'That's very soon. I don't know if I can be ready by then.'

'Nonsense! You've just come back from Cornwall, I understand, so you have holiday clothes with you. You and Hilly can go into Breverton tomorrow and buy what you need. Charge it to me.'

'But I couldn't possibly — ' the girl began to protest.

'Nonsense,' said Mrs Penn again. 'I'm rushing you, apparently, so I'll pay. Now then, Hilly, where's that young rascal Ian?'

'In London,' said Hilly, 'working on some new account.'

'So he's busy for a change. Good. I would have liked him to come with us, but if he's working hard for once we must leave him to it. When will he be back, do you think?'

163

Hilly shrugged. 'I've no idea.'

'Never mind. I'll be seeing his mother tomorrow, she'll tell me.' She got to her feet. 'I'm going to the study now. I want to make some notes.'

When she'd left the room on a waft of freesia perfume, the girls looked at each other and began to laugh.

'So we're off to Italy in three days.' Hilly sounded delighted.

'Didn't you know?' Jessica looked at her in surprise.

'No. I thought she was returning alone and that we would follow in a few weeks.'

'She's very forceful,' said Jessica.

'If by that you mean she likes her own way, then yes, she is. Now, are you happy to come into Breverton with me tomorrow or do you want to go home for clothes?'

'We'll have a shopping spree in Breverton,' said Jessica. 'It'll be fun. But I'm not sure about letting your mother foot the bill.'

Hilly waved a hand. 'Don't be silly.

She'll love to buy you things. We'll go straight after breakfast,' she decided. 'We'd better make lists of what we need.'

'I don't really need much,' said Jessica. 'Perhaps a sundress and some more sandals. I ruined mine on the rocks in Cornwall.'

They spent the evening happily making plans for their shopping spree the next day and for their two weeks in Italy.

'There's so much I want to show you,' said Hilly. 'It's the most beautiful place you can imagine.'

'I won't have much time for sight-seeing,' said Jessica. 'I'll be painting.'

'I think she wanted Ian to come with us,' said her friend. 'She's always matchmaking. I believe she thinks you'd do very nicely for him.'

Jessica's mouth dropped open. 'I know she writes romantic novels,' she said, 'but real life's not like a story. Ian will find his own girl.'

Hilly looked at her. 'You're in love

with him, aren't you?' she said quietly. 'You wish real life *was* like a story and could be plotted the way you want it to go.'

'We've discussed this before,' Jessica protested. 'I've told you how Ian feels.'

'But how do *you* feel?'

Jessica didn't answer at once. She stood up and strolled over to the window, looking out at the garden. How could she tell Hilly that she loved Ian as she had never loved anyone else? What if Hilly told him how she felt? She'd be mortified.

She turned round. 'Ian and I are just friends,' she said. 'If he comes to Italy, I'll have to make that quite plain to your mother.'

* * *

The shopping trip was a great success. Hilly was pleased to have Jessica's companionship and advice.

'I always shop with Mother,' she said, 'and I'm afraid what she likes me to wear is a bit well . . . old.'

Jessica studied her friend. Hilly always wore grey or black and not in the smartest styles. Her frankly rounded figure *couldn't* look elegant even in black. The thought occurred to her that perhaps Mrs Penn didn't want her to attract too much attention.

'Why don't you try a dress in aqua?' Jessica suggested. 'It would look so good with your light hair. Come on, let's see if they've got anything like that.'

They found just the dress for Hilly in a soft blue-green with tiny buttons on the bodice. Hilly gazed at her reflection in frank delight.

'I don't know what Mother will say, but I love it,' she declared.

Jessica looked at her handiwork with pleasure. 'Now we'll try coral pink,' she said.

Soon Hilly was gazing at her reflection in a dress of clear, bright pink.

'Oh, I'm so glad you came with me. I

look completely different!'

'Do you *want* to look different?' Jessica asked.

Hilly blushed. 'If I tell you something, promise not to tell Mother?'

'Of course,' said Jessica. 'My lips are sealed,' she said dramatically.

'Well . . . ' Hilly took a deep breath. 'I've got a boyfriend!'

Jessica looked at her in surprise. 'A boyfriend? But I've never seen you with anyone.'

'Not here. In Italy. His name is Alessandro.'

'And your mother doesn't know?'

'Oh no. She'd be cross. She's afraid I might leave her. I'm very useful as a secretary and assistant,' said Hilly.

'But that's wrong,' said Jessica. 'She could employ a secretary. You should be free to find someone you love. She should be happy for you.'

'You won't say anything, will you?' Hilly looked alarmed.

'I've promised. But do you want to look different for Alessandro?'

Hilly blushed again. 'He says he loves me as I am but I think he'd love me even more if I looked different — younger, more attractive.'

Jessica gave her friend a hug. 'He'll love you in your new dresses. Will I be able to meet him?'

'I want you to meet him,' said Hilly. 'It won't be easy. Mother keeps me very busy. But we'll work it out somehow. I'll say I want to show you the area around the villa. She can't object to that.' She gave Jessica a tremulous smile. 'Now let's find another beautiful dress for you.'

Jessica had imagined that Ramona Penn would like to see what the girls had bought, but when they returned to the house, she was leaving for dinner out with a friend.

Jessica shook out her new sundress and put it on a hanger.

'It's so pretty,' said Hilly admiringly. 'You'll be able to wear it without the little jacket in the sun and pop the jacket on in the evenings when it's cool.

And the blue and white stripes look so fresh. You're lucky to be able to wear fitted dresses like that.'

'Don't forget you have two pretty ones, too,' Jessica reminded her, and Hilly smiled happily.

'D'you know, its such a surprise, I'd almost forgotten. Now, shall we watch television or sit in the garden for a bit?'

'The garden,' said Jessica. 'It's a beautiful evening. And you can tell me some more about your Alessandro.'

* * *

Two days later, they left for the airport. Ramona Penn had so much luggage that there was barely room in the car for the girls' modest suitcases and Jessica's painting equipment.

'They're not all clothes,' Mrs Penn said defensively. 'That box is full of books, and that one has some old manuscripts I want to work on.'

Hilly laughed. 'That still leaves four cases of clothes,' she said. Her mother pretended not to hear.

As they pushed the two loaded luggage trolleys into the airport, Jessica looked back to see the novelist walking with a young man and talking earnestly.

Ian! She was talking to Ian.

'You mustn't neglect your work, but I would like you to join us for a few days if it's possible,' his aunt was saying as they joined the girls.

'Oh, it'll be possible,' Ian said cheerily. 'I'll come out on Friday then I can escort the girls home on the next weekend.'

'How did you know which flight we're taking?' Jessica asked as they walked towards the desk.

'Aunt Ramona told my mother and she told me when I rang home last night.'

'So you raced back from London to see us off.' Jessica gave him a little smile.

He slipped an arm round her shoulders. 'Of course.'

'And you're really coming out on Friday?'

Jessica's heart was singing with

happiness, but she tried to sound calm.

'My work went well in London, resulting in a new very promising contract, so I deserve a little holiday as a reward.'

Mrs Penn turned away from the check-in desk.

'We have quite a wait now,' she said to Ian. 'Can you stay with us? We'll choose some magazines then have a drink.'

'I'm sorry, Aunt Ramona, but I have to get back to the office. I just wanted to say *bon voyage*.'

He gave his aunt and Hilly a kiss and turned to Jessica. Hilly, seeing the hesitation on his face, tapped her mother's arm.

'Isn't that your friend Mrs Bruce over there?' She pointed across the concourse.

Ian, seizing the opportunity, bent and kissed Jessica swiftly on the cheek. 'See you on Friday,' he said and squeezed her hand.

'It's nothing like her,' Ramona Penn scolded her daughter. 'I think you need your eyes testing! Come along — the magazine shop is over there.'

Jessica moved off behind them. Ian had kissed her and she would see him again in a few days. Had he really come to see them all off or had he come to see her? She wished she knew. Was he beginning to regret being so dogmatic about not wanting to settle down?

If so, why didn't he tell her? Surely he couldn't think she still loved Gregory? Hadn't she made it plain that that was over? What could she do to make him realise she was interested in him?

Perhaps something would happen in Italy . . .

Beautiful Italy

Jessica stood on the balcony of her bedroom at the Villa Gardenia and breathed deeply. An appetising smell of garlic and tomatoes floated up from the kitchen in the basement. There always seemed to be a delicious smell of food in Italy, she thought. But mainly she was aware of the scent of flowers; flowers on balconies, flowers in tubs on the pavements, flowers in beds and borders.

Deep lilac bougainvillea climbed the villa walls and crept along her balcony. Magnolia trees with scented white petals, thick and rubbery, alternated with oleander bushes in pots, their petals white and pink.

Across the road from the villa, Lake Garda twinkled in the early morning sunshine, the pale green of the water contrasting with the backdrop of deep purple mountains. Villa and hotels strung along the shores of the lake were as colourful as the flowers in the gardens around them.

It was her third morning at the villa. She'd happily spent the first two days sketching and painting with barely a break, but Ramona Penn had decreed that Jessica must have a day off. So she was taking the two girls into Verona for the day and in the evening they were to go to the opera in the famous Roman amphitheatre.

Jessica didn't know yet if she liked opera, but she'd heard that performances at Verona were famous and a unique experience, so she found herself looking forward to it.

There was a knock at her bedroom door.

'Are you ready?' It was Hilly.

'Is it really time to leave? The lake is so beautiful this morning, I just want to gaze at it.'

Hilly glanced at her watch. 'If you like, I could tell Mother that we want to have coffee here before we leave. She won't mind. We'll find a lakeside cafe for you. In fact — ' she coloured ' — I have an idea.'

She was gone and Jessica turned again to her lake view. But in a few minutes, Hilly was back.

'Come on. We'll leave for Verona at ten.' She led the way downstairs and out of the villa.

Outside, Jessica closed her eyes and took a deep breath.

'Oh, Hilly, this place is so gorgeous, I don't know how you can bear to live anywhere else.'

Hilly laughed. 'I'm afraid that after a few months, you barely notice your surroundings. And it can get very hot here in summer. I'm glad to return for a few months to the gentler climate of England.'

They were walking along the promenade at the side of the lake. Hilly stopped outside a rather grand hotel.

'Wait here just a moment,' she said. 'I want to leave a message for someone.'

She was soon back. They continued walking a short distance then turned into a cafe with an imposing black and gold door. They sank into cream leather chairs around a table covered with a rose pink tablecloth. It was a glamorous, old fashioned cafe.

'I love the black and gold lamps,' said Jessica. 'They look Venetian.'

'Venice controlled this part of Lake Garda for many years,' said Hilly, 'so I suppose there would be a Venetian influence.'

'You seem to know a great deal about Italy.' said Jessica. 'Have you been coming here for many years?'

'Since I was a young teenager. My parents loved Italy. We came often and I was fascinated by the history and read up a lot. And of course I had to do research for Mother. And when she became famous, she bought the Villa Gardenia . . . '

'But you don't speak Italian, do you?'

'Only very badly. I was never any

good at languages.'

The waiter appeared with coffee and tiny sweet biscuits. Jessica sighed and looked out across the lake.

'What a perfect place. Imagine living here and seeing that view every day. You're so lucky, Hilly.'

'Even you would probably get tired of it eventually,' said Hilly.

'I wouldn't,' Jessica declared firmly. 'I would like a house right on the edge of the lake and to wake to see the water and the mountains and the flowers every morning.'

Hilly smiled indulgently. 'Drink up your coffee. We really must go soon. Tomorrow you can sit at the edge of the lake for as long as you like and sketch your perfect view.'

Jessica sipped her coffee and looked out at the lake. Wouldn't it be wonderful next week when Ian was here and they could enjoy this beauty together?

She became aware that Hilly was talking, but not to her.

'We've only got a few minutes. We're

spending the day and the evening in Verona.'

Jessica turned to see a young man standing beside Hilly; a young man with black curly hair and an olive complexion. He looked like a figure in an old Italian painting.

'Jessica, this is Alessandro.' There was a quiet pride on her face as she introduced him. 'This is my friend Jessica.'

Alessandro lifted Jessica's hand to his lips and gave a little bow.

'I am pleased to meet a friend of my Hilly,' he said, in heavily accented English.

'We have to go now,' said Hilly. 'Mother will be waiting.'

Jessica thought she heard the young man say to Hilly, 'I will see you later,' but Hilly shepherded her out of the cafe quickly and she couldn't be sure of the words.

'That was a short meeting,' she said to Hilly. 'Will I meet him again?'

'Perhaps sooner than you think,' said

Hilly with a mysterious smile. 'There's Mother. She's waiting for us.'

Mrs Penn climbed into an old-fashioned but comfortable Italian car and the girls followed. The driver moved off as soon as they were settled. He'd obviously been given his instructions in advance.

They were soon spinning along the road that skirted the bottom of Lake Garda. In time the road left the lake and for the next hour they sped in a straight line right into the heart of Verona.

'The city of opera and Shakespeare,' said Ramona Penn.

'The city of Romeo and Juliet,' said Jessica. 'I'd love to see Juliet's balcony.'

'We shall drop you here,' said Ramona. 'I'm spending the day at the Hotel Vittorio. They have the most wonderful spa facilities. I'll meet you both in the lounge at eight. It's quite near to the amphitheatre so we can walk across the square. Have a lovely day.'

Hilly and Jessica climbed out and the car sped away towards the city centre.

Hilly flung her arms in the air.

'Free!' she squealed with uncon-cealed joy. 'Free for a whole day!'

Jessica looked at her in amazement. What a strange reaction to her mother's departure.

'Come on,' said Hilly, glancing at her watch. 'We have twenty minutes.' She led the way down a narrow cobble-stoned alley and out into a vast square.

'Twenty minutes till what?' Jessica hurried to keep up with her friend. But Hilly didn't answer.

'What a huge arena,' said Jessica, as they began to cross the square and an imposing ruin loomed up in front of them. 'Just for death and gladiators. Weren't the ancient Romans a blood-thirsty lot?'

'It's used for peaceful spectacles now,' said Hilly. 'People come from all over the world to see the opera performances.'

'What do you think those huge figures are?' asked Jessica.

Enormous figures, over twenty feet tall, in fighting positions and wearing strange armour, stood ahead of them. Next to them was a row of sphinxes painted gleaming gold.

'Whatever can they be?' Jessica wondered.

'They're part of the sets and scenery for the operas,' explained an Italian lady who overheard them. She had also stopped to look at the figures. 'They are too big to store inside the arena and there are too many of them, so they leave them outside in the square until they are needed again. It is very interesting to watch the staff dragging huge parts of the set for one opera out and taking another lot in.'

She smiled as Jessica thanked her for the information.

Jessica was already rummaging in her sketching bag.

'Let me find somewhere to sit and sketch those figures. I'll never see anything like this again. Look, there's an open air cafe over there. Let's sit at a table at the front and we'll get a good view of the arena and the figures. It's time we had a coffee anyway.

'Oh, someone's got the best table,' she said, disappointed, but Hilly smiled at her.

'Don't worry.'

The man at the table stood up as they approached.

'*Buongiorno*, again,' said Alessandro, with a broad smile.

Jessica looked at Hilly and her friend smiled conspiratorially.

'Yes, we were making for this cafe all the time.'

He grinned, showing perfect white teeth. 'Now, what can I get you to drink? Cold fruit juice or coffee.'

They decided on fruit juice and he went to place the order.

'You planned to meet him this morning,' said Jessica. 'But what if your mother had been with us?'

'I knew she wouldn't be. She always goes to the spa hotel when we come to Verona.'

Alessandro appeared, followed by a waiter wearing a long white apron and bearing a tray aloft. Three tall glasses clinking with ice were placed on the table.

With a smile at Jessica, Hilly, looking charming in her new pink dress, took Alessandro to another table. Jessica grinned at them, spread out her sketch pad and pencils and began to draw.

From the other table came little whisperings and giggles, but, lost in her task, Jessica took no notice. Hilly was happy, that was enough for her.

They finished their drinks, and Jessica packed away her sketching things and put the little bag on her back.

'Have you seen anything of Verona yet?' Alessandro asked. 'I know it well. I could be your guide.'

'I'd love to see Juliet's balcony,' said Jessica.

'Come along then. You'll want to see the tomb, too. It's one of the sights of Verona.' He linked arms with the girls as they made their way out of the square.

The courtyard in front of Juliet's house was crowded, mostly with young people.

'It is always crowded,' said Alessandro.

There was a babble of voices, Italian, American, Japanese, and many more. They were calling up to the balcony, a carved stone box well above their heads. To Jessica's surprise, in answer to their calls, a young girl in Renaissance costume came out on to the balcony and waved graciously.

'More cinema than Shakespeare,' Alessandro muttered. 'I'm afraid the whole story is make-believe.'

'Oh, don't spoil it,' Hilly protested. 'People believe she was real. Look at the letters.'

On the wall opposite, little notes written on curling scraps of paper bore testimony to the belief of young lovers that the spirit of Juliet could make their dreams come true.

As they watched, a young Italian boy and girl walked slowly towards the balcony and looked up. They said nothing, but their wishes were in their fervent gaze and tightly clasped hands.

Jessica, Hilly and Alessandro went over to read some of the messages. Alessandro smiled at Hilly.

'Would you like to leave a message for Juliet about your lover?'

'I don't need to, do I?' As she gazed at him with shining eyes, he slipped an arm round her shoulders and pulled her close.

For a moment, Jessica felt bereft. If only Ian were here to put his arms round her. She wrapped her arms round herself, feeling very alone.

Alessandro noticed and slipped a hand through her arm.

'Come on, let's go and see the tomb.'

With Hilly on his other arm, they set off again and after a walk, reached the old building where the stone sarcophagus stood. Here there were no crowds, just a few people standing in respectful silence.

Jessica shivered despite the heat of the afternoon.

'I don't like this place.'

'So you don't want to sketch here?'

'No. I'd rather go.' The others agreed. It was very gloomy.

In the sunshine again, Jessica took a deep breath.

'What a pity the Romeo and Juliet story doesn't have a happy ending.'

'But it's only a story,' said Alessandro, 'despite what Verona would like us to believe. They didn't really exist, or not in the way Shakespeare portrays them.'

He put an arm round each girl's waist. 'What we need is a rest. We've been walking for quite a while in the sun. Let's find a bar for a long cool drink.'

★　★　★

The square outside the arena was pulsating with activity when they returned early in the evening. Jugglers caught a succession of balls in amazing rapidity. A fire-eater appeared to swallow huge mouthfuls of flames. Jessica shuddered and pulled her friends to where a crowd in the centre of the square surrounded a pair of dancers.

To the music of a strange wailing instrument, a girl in peasant costume and with bare feet skipped and twirled effortlessly. A slim young man with black curls and a wicked smile danced after her inside the circle of onlookers and, catching her, lifted her and swung her round and round. It was exhilarating to watch and they all clapped vigorously at the end and threw coins into the ring with the rest of the spectators.

'What time must you meet your mother?' asked Alessandro.

'At eight-thirty in the lounge of the Vittorio Hotel over there.'

The young man looked around. 'Shall we have an ice cream first?'

They strolled towards an ice cream cafe at the side of the square and gazed in amazement through the window, as an enormous dish, the size of a basin, was filled with fruit and cream and ice cream.

'Gracious, I couldn't eat that much,' protested Jessica.

'I could try,' said Hilly with a laugh.

'We'll ask for ordinary ones,' said Alessandro. 'These must be specials.'

They sat at a table and gave their orders.

'What time will the opera end?' asked Jessica.

'After midnight. It will be . . . ' The young man's voice tailed off as a tray was brought to their table. It bore three of the enormous glass dishes.

Jessica studied hers incredulously. 'I'll never eat all this ice cream,' she said faintly.

'I asked for ordinary ones,' said Alessandro. 'Perhaps they only sell enormous ones. I know we Italians are mad about ice cream, but really . . . '

'What a good thing we had a moderate dinner.'

Jessica picked up her spoon and plunged it gamely into the cream mountain.

'Oh, Hilly, it *is* gorgeous!'

189

* * *

The arena was huge. An elaborate set on many levels took up a third of the space. The rest of the area was given over to seats, on the ground level and in tiers rising to almost the top of the walls.

The tiers were packed tightly with people and there was a constant roar of voices talking and laughing.

Mrs Penn produced tickets and they were conducted to their seats. The girls looked at the huge stage area in amazement.

'The singers will be dwarfed by those figures,' said Jessica, looking at the gigantic gods and sphinxes. In the centre glowed an enormous golden pyramid.

A gong sounded. It was time for *Aida* to begin.

The crowd fell silent. Figures began to walk along the various levels of the stage and take up positions, dressed in brilliant coloured costumes; lines of people in vivid blue, groups in vibrant green, crowds in gold.

Lost in the drama of the story and the beauty of the music, she was surprised when the first act came to an end. Time had passed so quickly.

'Let's stretch our legs.' Hilly jumped up. They found a cool drink and took it outside where the audience was milling about in the square.

When they returned for the second act, it was to the magical sight of hundreds of pinpricks of light from little torches held by the audience in the tiers around the arena. Overhead, the blue velvety sky was pierced by twinkling stars, mirroring the lights below.

'It's absolutely magical,' breathed Jessica. 'I wouldn't have missed this for the world.'

The end came after midnight. With the emotional notes ringing in their ears of Aida and her lover's final tragic farewell, they made their way out into the blue Italian night. They were in a crowd of hundreds.

Around the square, dozens of brightly-lit cafes were busy. Despite the late hour, the pavement tables were crowded.

'We'll find some seats,' Mrs. Penn promised. 'We can't go back to the villa yet. We must finish off the evening in the proper Italian style.'

A few minutes later, Mrs Penn was leading them to a table outside a pretty bar.

'What would you like to eat?'

'Eat? I'm still full of ice cream.' Jessica protested. 'I'd enjoy a coffee — yet it's too warm for a hot drink.'

'I know just the thing.'

The waiter approached and Mrs Penn ordered a coffee for herself and two granitas.

'Granita?' queried Jessica.

The granita proved to be a glass full of crushed ice with coffee syrup poured over it. Jessica tasted it dubiously, then drank with enthusiasm.

'Delicious,' she declared. 'Just the thing for a warm evening.'

They sat back in their seats to watch the ever-changing drama in the square. Young lovers, arms entwined, strolled with eyes only for each other. Large family parties, from black-clad grandmothers to pretty little children, chattered past. Glamorous matrons carried pampered lapdogs.

Young men in crowds, but not in any way threatening, eyed up the girls who paraded, giggling, pretending not to notice them.

'Can you imagine all this going on in a square at home at this time of night?' said Jessica incredulously.

'They'd all be tucked up in bed,' Hilly agreed, finishing her granita.

'This has been a wonderful day,' said Jessica to her companions. 'Thank you so much for bringing me to Verona.'

'You couldn't return home without seeing it,' replied Mrs Penn. 'But now I think we should leave. The villa is an hour's drive away.'

* * *

Jessica was silent on the return journey. Love was everywhere in this magical country, she thought. Romeo and Juliet, Aida and Radames, Hilly and Alessandro, Jessica and . . . who? Certainly not Jessica and Gregory. Jessica and Ian? No, that too had to be ruled out.

She felt tears begin to prick her eyes and closed them, pretending to be dozing. If Hilly spoke to her, she couldn't trust herself not to sound emotional.

'May I come in and talk for a few moments?' Hilly asked as they made their way to their bedrooms.

Jessica was tired. She wanted to be alone, to think back over the wonderful evening, but she couldn't refuse. She knew Hilly wanted to talk about Alessandro.

'Well?' asked Hilly. 'What do you think of him?'

Jessica smiled. 'I think he's quite charming,' she replied.

'And handsome?'

'Very handsome,' Jessica agreed solemnly.

Hilly sank on to the bed. 'I love him,'

she said simply, 'but it's no use. Mother won't approve.'

'Why not? I can't believe she just wants to keep you as a — a slave! Is he already married? Is he very poor?'

Hilly gave a little laugh. 'He's not married and he's certainly not poor. You know the Hotel Monte Rosa where I went this morning? His father owns it. And another hotel in Milan.'

Jessica was silent for a moment then she said, 'I should have thought your mother would find him a very suitable match.'

'You mean money-wise? That doesn't carry any weight with Mother. She has plenty of her own. She just wants to keep me with her.'

'Where did you meet him?' asked Jessica.

'At a reception at the hotel. Most of the guests were Mother's contemporaries. Alessandro and I were the youngest there so we got talking. Italian men like curvy girls.' She giggled. 'We found each other attractive. We managed to meet quite often when Mother was busy and we phone and write when I'm in England. But as for the future . . . ' She sighed hopelessly.

Jessica tried to hide a yawn and immediately Hilly stood up. 'I'm sorry, Jessica, you're tired. I'll go. See you in the morning.'

Jessica began to undress. Poor Hilly. If only there was someone to persuade Mrs Penn. But would she listen to anyone? She was a very strong-willed lady.

Jessica got into bed. She would have to think about the problem. For now, she just wanted to sleep.

'Surprise!'

Jessica set up her easel early the next morning, refreshed by her day away from painting. The picture was two-thirds finished. The villa with its creamy golden walls and ochre roof glowed in the early morning sun. The air was sweet.

She looked up towards Hilly's balcony. The green shutters were still fastened. Hilly was still asleep, probably dreaming of Alessandro.

For a moment, Jessica thought about the young Italian. If only she could do something to help the romance. They were obviously in love and well suited to each other, but how could anyone make Ramona Penn put her daughter's happiness before her own convenience?

Jessica sighed and picked up her brush again, blending shades of cream and grey to add the balconies at the side of the villa.

By the time she heard the rattle of shutters and saw Hilly yawning on her balcony, Jessica had added all the shutters to the side of the house and was starting to mix blue and green for the bay trees and olive trees in the lush gardens around the villa.

'Jessica,' called Hilly. 'Whatever are you doing? Have you had your breakfast?'

'Only a cup of coffee,' Jessica called back. 'I wanted to get on with the painting. I'll be down in ten minutes. We can have breakfast together.'

The girls ate on the terrace in the shady garden at the back of the villa. It was beginning to get hot and Jessica was glad of the striped awnings overhead.

She was slightly dismayed to see Ramona Penn already seated at the table. The novelist had been very kind to her, but Jessica couldn't help being rather in awe of her. She had hoped to have her meal with just Hilly for company.

The early morning air had given her an appetite and she tucked into the flaky golden croissants and cherry jam with enthusiasm.

'I believe the painting is almost finished.' Ramona fixed Jessica with her direct stare. 'When may I see it?'

'After breakfast, if you like,' said the girl. 'There are a few parts to complete but it's almost finished.'

'No,' Ramona decided. 'I shall wait until tomorrow. Will it be done by then? I want to see a perfect picture.'

When she had left the table, Jessica turned to Hilly and made a little face. 'Perfect! No pressure then! Will she think it's perfect, do you think?'

'She loves the English one,' Hilly pointed out. 'Don't worry, I'm sure she'll be delighted.'

Jessica went back to her work, determined that Ramona Penn would have no cause for complaint.

The next morning, soon after breakfast, Jessica set up her easel in the salon and displayed her painting. Hilly had already seen it and was most impressed. Now they waited for Ramona Penn.

The author scrutinised the painting. She stepped away from it, then forward again until she was just a foot or so away. Then she sighed.

'I'm very pleased,' she pronounced. 'It's perfect. It will make a wonderful pair with the English one. I shall hang them each side of the fireplace in this room.'

Relieved, Jessica smiled at Hilly who gave her an 'I told you so' nod.

'Now then — ' Ramona seated herself on the wide cream sofa and patted the place beside her, looking at Jessica. 'Come and sit here. Would you be prepared to paint other houses if you were asked?'

'I'd hoped I might get some further commissions,' Jessica admitted.

'Then tomorrow evening we shall have a little reception here,' said the novelist. 'And I shall invite all my acquaintances to view the painting. Then we'll see.'

Jessica beamed. 'That's very kind of you, Mrs Penn. I'm so pleased you like it.'

'I hope that young rascal Ian will be here by then. He can help to entertain the guests.'

★   ★   ★

However Ian had not arrived by eight when the guests began to drift through the warm, flower-perfumed night to the villa.

Ramona, stately in black with gold rings and chains, conducted them to the painting. The English house stood on another easel to the rear.

Jessica, suddenly shy, sat with Hilly at the back of the room but was brought forward to stand with Ramona by the easel.

The picture was much admired, and an hour later she had received five commissions to paint other lakeside villas. Glowing with pride, she rejoined Hilly.

'Five commissions,' she gloated. 'Five!'

'And the evening's not over yet,' said Hilly.

'I must go and find a drink.' Jessica

stood up. 'So much talking has made me dry. Would you like one?'

Hilly shook her head.

Jessica left the warmth and chatter of the salon and crossed the cool marble hall. Glancing to her left, she saw a figure sitting on the stairs. He gazed at her solemnly.

'Ian! We didn't know you were here. What are you doing sitting there?'

'Waiting for you. You know this is where we spend our time at parties.'

'Idiot!' Jessica giggled. 'Why didn't you tell us you were here like a normal person?'

'Because if I was just a normal person, you wouldn't notice me. I try really hard to be a bit different.'

'When did you arrive?'

'Half an hour ago. Everything was in full swing so I was able to creep in the back way and up to my room to change. Is the picture finished?'

'Yes. This reception is for all Mrs Penn's friends to see it — and hopefully commission me to paint their houses.'

'And . . . ?'

'Five commissions already,' Jessica said gleefully. 'Everyone seems to like it.'

'You're a very clever girl. Now, are you going to come and sit on the stairs with me or are you going to stand there all evening?'

'I'm supposed to be getting some drinks,' she said, 'and you must go and speak to your aunt. She was wondering whether you were still coming.'

'OK.' He rose reluctantly. 'I'll see you back here in ten minutes.'

He entered the salon and Jessica went into the kitchen to find some drinks.

Ten minutes later, they were again sitting on the stairs. Ian wriggled happily. 'I think this is my favourite place for a chat. Now tell me what's been happening.'

'Well, you already know about the painting. Then your aunt took us for a day in Verona and we ended up watching a fantastic performance of Aida.'

'Lucky you. I wish I'd been there. It's

my favourite opera.'

A sudden thought struck Jessica. Perhaps Ian could help Hilly.

'Something strange happened before we went,' she said. 'I was introduced to Hilly's boyfriend.'

'Her *boyfriend*?' He sounded genuinely startled.

'Yes. Alessandro.'

'Why did I know nothing of him before this?'

'Nobody knew,' said Jessica. 'They've been friendly for over a year but nothing's been said because your aunt wouldn't approve.'

'Why? What's wrong with him?'

'Nothing's wrong. He's very nice and thinks the world of Hilly. But Mrs Penn wants to keep Hilly with her. She thinks she's irreplaceable as secretary, PA, assistant and so on.'

Ian thought for a while. 'So Aunt Ramona has never met him? Perhaps I can help. Where's Hilly now?'

★ ★ ★

204

The reception was deemed a great success. With five firm commissions and two possible ones, Jessica was thrilled and excited.

'You must stay here when you come back to do them,' Hilly told her. 'When do you think it will be?'

Jessica couldn't say; she still had aspects of her private life to sort out, but the two girls made hopeful plans for the future.

'Now the picture is finished, there's nothing to keep me here for the moment,' said Jessica regretfully. 'I suppose I'll be going back to England in a few days.'

'I'm coming with you,' said Hilly. 'I still have books and papers to sort at home and I need to be there to supervise the building of the new bathroom.'

'Will Ian come back with us?' asked Jessica, trying not to sound too hopeful.

'I'm sure he will. He only came for a few days.'

Two evenings later, as Jessica, Hilly

and her mother were enjoying pre-dinner drinks, Ian strode in followed by a dark-haired young Italian man. Hilly gave a gasp.

'Aunt Ramona,' said Ian. 'I'm sure you won't mind but I've brought a friend to dinner.'

Ramona Penn gave Alessandro a gracious smile and extended her hand. 'Welcome, Mr — er — '

'Just Alessandro,' he said softly.

'Alessandro,' she repeated. 'It will be interesting to have someone new at dinner. Do you live locally or are you staying at Garda?'

Jessica and Hilly exchanged nervous smiles. Ian ignored them.

'Alessandro is the *only* — ' he emphasised the word ' — son of Senor Calvi of the Monte Rosa Hotel.'

'Indeed.' Mrs Penn was interested. 'Tell me, how long have you known my nephew?'

Before the Italian could answer, Ian brought Jessica and Hilly forward and introduced them. Her mother appeared not to notice Hilly's flaming cheeks.

When the dinner gong sounded they found another place had been laid at the table and Ian contrived to seat his cousin next to Alessandro.

The dinner was a success. Ramona Penn was charmed by the handsome young Italian.

'You must come to dinner again very soon,' she said.

'What a perfectly charming young man,' she told the girls when they were alone. 'I think he could be a good influence on Ian.'

When her mother had left the room, Hilly turned to Jessica. 'How did Ian know about Alessandro? Did you tell him?'

'Yes, and you should be glad that I did,' said Jessica before she could protest. 'Things can develop from here. Ian has given you a fine start.'

The door opened and Ian came into the room.

'Well, am I a clever boy?'

Hilly ran to him and flung her arms

207

round his neck. 'You are. You really are.'

'Don't forget Jessica's part in this. If she hadn't told me . . . '

'If he continues to charm your mother like he has, you'll soon be announcing your engagement,' said Jessica with a laugh. 'I'm sure he'll appear as the hero in her next romance.'

They were toasting their success and laughing merrily when Ramona Penn came back into the room.

'Am I missing something? What are we celebrating?' she asked.

'Oh . . . we're just feeling happy,' said Ian, pouring her a drink. 'Jessica has her commissions, you have a new hero for your next book — and Hilly just might have found herself a beau,' he added wickedly.

'Don't worry about Hilly,' said his aunt. 'What about your future? When are you going to find yourself some-one?'

Ian crossed his legs and gazed at the toe of his shoe.

'Well, Aunt, it's just possible I've found someone, too.'

'Really? Tell us about her. Is it someone we know?'

'My lips are sealed. Even the lady herself doesn't know it yet.' He yawned. 'Excuse me. It's been a long day. I'm off to bed. I'll see you all in the morning.' And he left the room, Jessica staring after him.

★ ★ ★

The next morning, Jessica followed her practice of getting up early and going to sit at the side of the lake. With no painting to do, she had taken a pad and sketching pencils. She was making a rapid impression of the little boats busily crossing from bank to bank.

When Ian at last emerged on to his balcony he was pleased to see Jessica sitting alone on the terrace below. For a moment, he enjoyed the picture she made. Then he leaned over the railings.

'Jessica!' He called and waved.

'Shouldn't I be up there and you down here?' she asked with a laugh.

'That's only in Verona. Don't go away, I'll be right down.'

A few minutes later, he slipped into the seat opposite.

'What a lovely morning.' He sniffed the air appreciatively. 'You can see right to the far bank of the lake. Have you eaten?'

'Of course. This air gives you an appetite. I couldn't wait. I had breakfast with the others.'

Ian gestured to the maid and ordered coffee and croissants and another cup for Jessica.

'You must have something to keep me company,' he said in answer to her protests. He looked around. 'Where are Aunt Ramona and Hilly?'

'They've gone for a boat trip on the lake. They'll be out all day.'

'Leaving you on your own?'

'I wanted to sketch.'

He looked pleased. 'A little bird tells me that Aunt Ramona might have a reason for leaving you alone,' he said enigmatically.

The maid appeared so she was saved the embarrassment of answering. But she felt sure he was right. His aunt was throwing them together.

She thought of what he'd said last night. Perhaps his aunt didn't believe him.

He held out his hand for her sketchpad. 'May I?'

He studied it for a few moments. Jessica had drawn the large white lake steamer as it passed their hotel.

'Very good, especially as it was moving.' He refilled their cups. 'Would you like to go on the steamer? It crosses to the narrow peninsula opposite us several times a day. There's a very pretty town at the end. Plenty to draw over there.'

* * *

It was pleasantly cool on the lake. A breeze blew Jessica's hair back from her

211

face as she stood at the front of the boat, gazing entranced at the picturesque scene ahead. The water's edge was crowded with houses and hotels in cream and white with ochre roofs. In the gardens, poplars and cypresses stood among thick beds of vivid scarlet flowers. There was a small castle at one end of the town and a church at the other.

'It's like a jigsaw puzzle picture,' Jessica cried. 'It's so pretty!'

They disembarked on to a little jetty and made their way into the town which was small and quaint. Jessica was beginning to get used to the shops which filled the little Italian towns. There were leather shops selling bags and wallets; shoe shops full of jewelled, strappy sandals; windows full of bright but rather garish pottery; fruit shops, their fresh strawberries and apricots glistening in the sun, and, of course, ice cream parlours. One shop boasted over one hundred flavours.

After a drink, they decided to follow

a path which ran alongside the lake. Wooden seats positioned at intervals, gave Jessica the chance to sit and record the scene in front of her. She was glad that Ian had brought a book.

'I'm prepared, like the boy scouts,' he said. 'I thought we might be making lots of stops.'

'Just look at those little birds,' Jessica exclaimed. 'They look like sparrows. They're paddling in the ripples at the water's edge.'

Ian took a few photographs of the birds and they strolled on. Jessica decided it was one of the most pleasant days she'd ever spent.

They ate a typical Italian lunch of pasta with tomato sauce, then wandered along the lakeside with an ice cream, sitting first on one seat then another so that Jessica could draw until her hand ached.

'When I was at art school, I longed for a sketching holiday abroad,' she confided to Ian.

'But you never came?'

'No. No money. I'd used it all up at college. But I planned to come one day.' She gave him a happy smile. 'I never dreamed it would be like this. I know I came to work, but it's been a perfect holiday.'

He smiled ruefully. 'I wish we could stay longer. I can't believe we have to go back tomorrow.'

'You're leaving tomorrow, too?'

'Yes. I can't leave my business for too long.'

A few minutes later, they made their way back into the town.

'I want to buy a few presents,' Jessica commented.

'Me too,' he agreed.

They spent a pleasant hour selecting gifts; handbags for their mothers and a wallet for Jessica's father.

'What time will Aunt Ramona and Hilly be back?' Ian asked.

'Late. They're spending the evening at a nightclub. Mrs Penn wants some colour for her new book. I believe Alessandro is escorting them.'

'Again leaving you on your own.'

She blushed. 'I think your aunt thinks we might . . . '

'Like to be alone?' he finished. He took her hand. 'We mustn't disappoint them. Shall we go back to the villa? You'll have time to rest before we go out this evening.'

She looked surprised. 'Where are we going?'

'Not far away. To a beautiful restaurant overlooking the lake where we can dine and dance. So wear your most glamorous dress.'

'Oh, dear, is it very grand? I haven't anything really glamorous.'

'I don't believe it. Anything you wear will look beautiful. No, it's not grand, just unusual. I'm sure you'll like it.'

The car park for the restaurant was well above the lake. They parked and made their way down steps and a little path which twisted between shady trees to the restaurant below. From the lake, the restaurant seemed to be almost concealed under overhanging trees.

Huge blocks of stone made an unusual bar serving area. The chef presided over an open fire oven which glowed mysteriously in the dusk of the evening.

Wrought iron chairs were thickly cushioned and the table cloths, which reached to the ground were a soft sage green. A waterfall cascaded down rocks at the back of the dining-room and bubbled into a pool below.

They were led to a table overlooking the lake. Jessica looked round in delight.

'I feel as if I'm sitting in an underwater cave,' she said. The waiter brought iced water and silver bowls of bread. Ian studied the menu.

'Do you like duck?' he asked.

'Love it.'

'Would you like me to order for you?'

'All right. It'll make me try something different from what I usually choose. But nothing too strange,' she said. 'I'm not very adventurous with food.'

216

He selected risotto with different types of mushrooms and then the duck which was garnished with grapes.

'The best duck I've ever tasted,' Jessica said when she finished the last morsel, and Ian looked pleased.

'Would you like to dance now?' he asked, and she looked around in surprise.

'But there's no dance floor.'

'Through there.' Ian pointed to an archway in the wall. Jessica hadn't noticed it.

'I'd love to.'

Ian courteously pulled back her chair and placed an arm round her waist to lead her to the dance floor.

'I love your dress,' he said. 'I thought you said you hadn't anything glamorous.'

Jessica flushed. 'I suppose I should say, 'this old thing'', she said with a smile. 'I've had it a while but it's one of my favourites.'

'The colour sets off the tan you're acquiring. If only you were staying longer. You won't be able to top it up in the rain of an English summer.'

They'd reached the archway and stepped through. The dance floor was small and circular and paved with blue, green and white mosaic tiles. Three musicians played in a little alcove at the side. There were already three couples dancing so it seemed quite crowded.

She went into Ian's arms.

'Very intimate,' he whispered. 'I like small dance floors.'

Jessica thought back to the last time she'd danced with him, at Hilly's party. He was remembering it, too.

'I shan't sing,' he promised.

Jessica gazed up at the blue velvet sky and the twinkling stars. She thought she would remember this night for ever.

She knew she was in love with Ian and that it was pointless. He'd made it quite plain that theirs was just a friendship albeit a flirtatious one. And what about the mysterious girl he had mentioned to his aunt. He might just have been teasing — Jessica hoped he was. She couldn't bear to think of him with someone else.

But what of her resolution to ignore romance and concentrate on her career? Hadn't she had enough heartache with Gregory? But there was no comparison between the two men. Gregory was quite attractive but Ian was handsome and desirable. Gregory could be petty and diffident. Ian was confident and lighthearted. And he was knowledgeable but never a bore.

Everything I want in a man, she told herself dejectedly.

Ian had been watching the different expressions flit across her face. He wondered whether she was tired of dancing.

'Shall we return to the table?' he asked. 'We can dance again later if you like.'

They returned to plates of Italian cheeses and bowls of fresh fruit; grapes, cherries, peaches and strawberries, sitting on a bed of crushed ice.

On the water, a steamer ablaze with

lights made a slow progress up the far side of the lake.

'Is a night steamer,' said the waiter as he removed dishes from the table. 'You can eat and look at the villages as you pass. Many have floodlit buildings. Is very pretty and — ' he gave a knowing smile ' — romantic.'

They ordered coffee. Jessica didn't really want any but she was reluctant to leave this romantic place and destroy the atmosphere between them.

They returned to the dance floor. The music was soft and sweet. Jessica closed her eyes.

'Wake up,' Ian whispered. 'I don't think I could carry you up all those steps to the car. Though I'd try,' he added gallantly.

'I wasn't asleep,' she protested. 'But it's so comfortable turning round and round to the music. It's a lovely feeling when you close your eyes. Try it.'

'I don't think we should both close our eyes,' he said. 'We might fall off the dance floor and into the lake.'

Jessica giggled. The music ceased and the musicians left their alcove.

'There's another night steamer,' said Jessica as they resumed their seats. She rummaged in her bag and produced a small sketching tablet.

Opposite her, Ian glanced at what she was doing then turned to the view in front of them. He seemed lost in a reverie.

Jessica chose a pencil and began to sketch rapidly. She worked without speaking. Ian continued to look out at the lights on the opposite bank of the lake. Suddenly he stood up and came to stand behind her.

'Let me see what you've made of the scene . . . ' He stared at the sketch with an enigmatic expression. There was no way to conceal what she'd done. Jessica, who'd hoped to whip the pad away before he saw it, sat in silence as he considered his own likeness.

'I preferred this view,' she said quietly.

'That's quite a compliment.' He

returned to his seat to gaze at her across the table. The colour rose softly to her cheeks. Hastily she replaced the pad in her bag.

'I think I'd like to go now,' she said and stood up to cover her confusion.

In the car, he carefully made no move to touch her. They sat in silence, then, 'We said just friends,' he reminded her.

'Of course,' she agreed, too hastily.

'You're still officially engaged to Gregory. I can't take advantage. You're in a vulnerable state at the moment. How would we feel if, when you return home, you decided to go back to Gregory?'

'I'm not sure what this conversation means,' she said, 'but don't try to explain. Let's go back to the villa.'

He turned the key in the ignition and the car moved off.

'What time do we leave tomorrow?' she asked after a while. She knew it was one o'clock but the topic was the only thing that came to mind to put the conversation back on a safe footing.

They began to chat about the journey home to England and very soon had reached the villa.

'Would you like to join me for a nightcap?' he asked. 'Everyone else seems to be in bed.'

She was tempted. It would prolong the evening. But then she remembered the way he'd reacted to her sketch of him. She had given away her feelings; he'd made his quite plain. She felt that when they returned to England they would remain just friends — or part for ever.

'I have some packing to do,' she said. 'I don't want to leave it all for the morning. Thank you, Ian, for a wonderful evening.'

He looked down at her, saying nothing. Then he put his hands on her shoulders and bent to kiss her forehead. As she raised her eyes to his, their lips met.

'Thank you, Jessica. I enjoyed it so much. I'll see you in the morning.' He watched as she climbed the stairs, pausing to wave to him from the top, then went thoughtfully down to the salon. He poured himself a drink and took it out into the garden.

Had it been a good idea to follow Jessica to Lake Garda? Of course it had. He'd had two wonderful evenings with her. But feelings had become tense. He sat down on a bench and sighed.

If only he knew whether she really wanted to part from Gregory. He had first call on her. Technically, they were still engaged. How could he, Ian, reveal his own true feelings? He tossed back his drink and stood up. The moment he was certain that Jessica was free, he would claim her for his own.

★ ★ ★

They all took breakfast together the next morning. Jessica and Ian were rather quiet. They each wanted to discuss the evening before, the unusual restaurant, the food, the dancing, but that would remind them of the end of the evening and that was too emotional. And it couldn't be discussed in front of other people.

So they all talked of the lake, the weather and what they would be doing next week.

'How many photos have you taken?' asked Jessica.

'I don't know. Why?'

'For a photo journalist, you don't seem to use your camera much.'

He looked at her quizzically. 'How do you know what I was doing when you were busy sketching?'

She smiled and shrugged her shoulders. Ian tried to mention the drawing she had made of him, but she changed the subject. The incident was too embarrassing. Then the meal was finished and they parted to finish their packing.

In her bedroom, Jessica gazed from her window at the azure water and the flowers.

'It's too beautiful to leave,' she said to Hilly who had come into the room. And to think that it would be here, unchanging, while she was in England, probably in the rain, and certainly with none of the beauty of this region. But the scene was locked into her mind. She had only to close her eyes and she could recall it whenever she liked.

'You'll be back one day,' Hilly reminded her. 'You have all the paintings to do. And perhaps you'll come back with Ian.' She gave Jessica a knowing smile.

Jessica, Hilly and Ian travelled to the airport and checked in. They found seats for the wait until their flight was called.

'They may have an English newspaper on that stand,' said Ian. 'I'll go and see.'

He was soon back carrying two newspapers.

'They have some English and American magazines, too,' he told the girls.

'I'll wander over and have a look. It'll fill some time. Are you coming, Hilly?'

Hilly shook her head. She'd brought

books and had settled down to wait.

Jessica selected a glossy magazine and was turning to walk back to her seat whcn she caught her foot in the dangling strap of a bag on a luggage trolley. Losing her balance, in a second she had crashed to the ground, agonising pain shooting through her ankle.

The owner of the bag flung was distraught.

'Someone get help!' he shouted. 'Oh, I'm so sorry. It was completely my fault.'

Jessica couldn't speak for the pain in her ankle.

Within a few moments, two paramedics appeared and took charge, examining her ankle thoroughly to ensure it wasn't broken, then lifting her easily between them and seating her in a wheelchair.

Ian and Hilly were unaware of the drama being enacted at the magazine stall and looked up, startled, as Jessica appeared alongside them in a wheelchair.

'What on earth . . . ?'

One of the paramedics quickly

explained the situation.

'If you will wait here, miss, we will return when your flight is called and help you aboard.'

The others were concerned but there was nothing they could do.

'Such a silly accident,' Jessica said, biting her lip. 'Such a nuisance.'

'Don't worry about it. I can carry your hand luggage.'

The owner of the bag came over, looking concerned. 'It isn't broken, is it?'

'It'll be fine,' said Jessica through tight lips. 'Please don't worry.'

'The young lady will be fine,' said Ian. 'She just wants to sit quietly for a while.' He put a hand on the man's arm and turned him away from Jessica.

'Perhaps he thinks I'm going to sue him,' said Jessica grumpily.

Before Ian could answer, their flight was called. The paramedics re-appeared and Jessica found herself being wheeled to the head of the boarding queue.

An attendant settled her in her seat

as comfortably as possible.

'Let me know if you need anything else,' she said with a friendly smile.

Ian took the seat next to her and reached out to grasp her hand.

'Poor girl,' he said. 'Does it hurt very much?'

She held his hand tightly. 'A bit. It happened so quickly, there was nothing I could do. What will happen when I get back to England?'

'I'll take you back to Hilly's and you can decide how bad your ankle is and where you want to go.'

All Her Heart

'It was very kind of you to invite me to stay with you.' Jessica smiled at Hilly and hobbled from the table to an armchair.

'You couldn't have managed at the guest house,' said Hilly, gathering their dinner plates on to a tray. 'I'll put these in the dishwasher then we'll have some coffee.' She left the room and Jessica made herself comfortable with her injured foot on a stool. Fortunately the paramedics had been correct in their assessment that it wasn't broken, but although it was much better it was still tender.

She'd been back from Italy for two days and her mind was still in a turmoil. She wanted Ian with all her heart. She knew that she loved him as she had never loved anyone before, but she had to accept that he didn't love her.

He'd made it plain from the beginning of their friendship that he wanted no commitment.

But her mind kept returning to incidents in Italy; the way he'd held her hand on the plane, the feel of his arms enfolding her as they danced. Was it just flirtation? Did he really feel nothing towards her?

She closed her eyes and wished, not for the first time, that she'd never met him. Love was wonderful, but it was agony when it was unrequited.

Suddenly she knew she couldn't see him again. It was torture to be near him and to know he only wanted her as a friend when she wanted him as . . .

She couldn't admit it even to herself. Once she said the word she was lost. There was only one thing for it, she must go home.

In a flash, she knew that was what she wanted. She would go home and never see Ian again. Hilly would soon be in Italy again and there would be no need to return here. She had all the details she needed of the commissions in Italy. She would deal with them in the future.

Hilly returned with a tray of coffee and put it down on a little table, and was surprised by the other girl's bright smile.

'I've made a decision,' said Jessica. 'I'm going home to my flat tomorrow.'

'But your foot! You can't drive yet. Perhaps I could . . . '

'No! You've done enough. You can't spare the time to drive me home when you have only a short time left to finish your sorting and packing.'

'But you can't drive . . . ' Hilly began in protest.

'Bind it up for me in the morning,' said Jessica. 'It isn't broken, it just needs support. I'll drive carefully and make stops to rest it. I'll be fine.'

Hilly was silent, thinking. Then she said, 'Perhaps Ian . . . '

'No!' Jessica almost shouted. Then more quietly: 'Don't say anything to Ian. I just want to go home quietly. Promise you won't call him.'

Hilly hesitated doubtfully, then nodded. 'All right — but I'm not happy about it.

Won't you stay a few days longer? Your ankle will be stronger then.'

'Hilly,' said Jessica quietly, 'I want to go home. The last few weeks have been tiring in many ways. I just want to work quietly in my own surroundings.'

Her friend reached across and patted her hand.

'If that's what you really want, I'll say no more. Now, shall we watch the film on television? It has four stars.'

'I don't think so. I'm going to pack my bags ready for the morning.'

She hobbled out of the room and up the stairs.

Of course, she hadn't told Hilly the truth. Her foot was hurting quite badly and driving would be uncomfortable, but she was determined to leave. She just couldn't bear to see Ian again. She needed to go home and forget him.

She had packed her clothes and was carefully sorting her painting equipment when she became aware of voices downstairs. She crept out on to the landing.

Hilly was talking to a man. Ian! Her heart beat wildly. Just when she'd made her decision about him.

She moved back into the bedroom as Hilly ran up the stairs.

'It's Ian. He wants to see you.'

'Tell him I'm in bed asleep,' said Jessica.

'I can't do that.' Hilly sounded upset. 'You know I'm no good at fibs. Please, Jessica, come down and see him.'

As Jessica said nothing, Hilly suddenly burst out, 'I can't make you out. You said you had a good time in Italy. You spent a lot of time with Ian. Now you won't speak to him. What's going on?'

Jessica sighed. 'All right — I'll come.'

Ian's face lit up when he saw her, then his expression changed to one of concern. 'Still hobbling. Is it no better?'

'It's fine,' said Jessica, with attempted brightness. 'Just a bit stiff.'

The sight of him brought back all her feelings of earlier in the evening. She must stick to her resolve not to see him again.

He seemed unaware of her mood and turned to his cousin.

'I hope you've seen Jessica's sketches. She'll be able to build some of them into really good pictures.'

Hilly turned to the sideboard and poured three glasses of wine. Jessica took one reluctantly, but Ian smiled as he took his.

'What shall we drink to? How about Hilly's trip to Italy. May it go well.'

'And to Jessica's trip home tomorrow,' said Hilly quietly.

Ian turned a shocked face to Jessica. 'You're going home tomorrow? So soon?'

'Well . . . Hilly will be leaving soon, and I can't stay then.'

'But you can't drive with an injured ankle. I have an idea. Come and stay with Mother and me. She'd love to have you.'

'It's very kind of you, but no thank you. I need to go home.' To be under the same roof as Ian again would revive all the agonised feelings she'd had such difficulty repressing.

Ian turned to his cousin. 'Can't you persuade her, Hilly?' he appealed. 'She can't drive home on her own with an injured foot.'

'Believe me, I've tried,' said Hilly. 'But she insists on going.'

'Very well,' said Ian, sounding very assertive, 'if you insist on going, I insist on driving you. No — ' he raised a hand as she opened her mouth to argue ' — there's no more to be said. Tell me what time you want to leave and I'll be here.'

'But how will you get home? It will be so inconvenient for you.'

'Bus, train, hire car — what does it matter? What matters is getting you safely home.'

Jessica had never yet got the better of Ian in a argument. She gave in.

They agreed that he should be at Hilly's house at twelve the next day to drive her home in her own car.

Jessica went to bed with very mixed feelings, torn between joy at another day with Ian and despair that his closeness on the journey would increase her unhappiness.

When he leaves me at the flat, that will definitely be the last time I see him, she told herself as she switched off her bedside lamp.

She lay staring into the darkness, remembering the first time they met. Then, she had been the one to hold him at arm's length, determined not to get involved. Now the tables were turned.

'Oh, Ian,' she breathed, 'I love you. Why can't you love me?'

* * *

The journey home took less than an hour. They talked of their holiday, but carefully, discussing the artwork they'd seen, the Italian countryside, the delicious ice cream, but avoiding any topics that would recall their closeness. She was aware of his puzzled looks now and again, but made sure there were no long gaps in the conversation to allow him to introduce any subjects that would increase her discomfort. He'd made it clear he wanted only friendship, nothing would induce her to let him see that she wanted more.

She tried to laugh, to joke, to sound bright, but it was an effort and she was glad when they turned into the road where she had her flat.

'Let's have a coffee first,' she suggested, 'then perhaps you would bring up my bags. Drive in here — you can leave your car at the side of the house.'

The large Edwardian house was divided into six flats. Jessica's was on the first floor. Ian helped her up the stairs and they stopped outside a yellow painted door. Jessica had the key in her hand, but from within the flat they could hear soft bumps and bangs. She frowned, puzzled.

He took the key and motioned her to stand behind him. Then, quietly, he turned it in the lock and pushed open the door.

Jessica, looking over his shoulder, saw

a man standing in the middle of the room, a pile of CDs in his hand.

'Gregory! What are you doing here? How dare you break into my flat? Get out at once.'

'Break in? You gave me a key.'

'A key you have no right to use now.'

Gregory seemed to notice Ian for the first time.

'No, I can see it must be embarrassing for my replacement,' he said spitefully.

'I'm not embarrassed,' said Ian cheerfully. 'And I'm not a replacement.'

Gregory looked him up and down. 'So who are you?'

'Just a friend helping out.'

'A friend? I've never met you before.'

'A new friend,' said Ian with a smile. He held out a hand. 'Ian Grantly.'

Gregory ignored the hand and bent down to pick up another pile of CDs. Jessica felt it time to break up this exchange.

'Please go,' she said to Gregory. 'I don't know what you think you're doing here.'

'Collecting what belongs to me.'

'I'll sort out your CDs and books and put them in a box,' she said. 'You can call for them at the weekend.'

Gregory opened his mouth to say something but the icy glare on her face changed his mind. He picked up his car keys and made for the door.

Ian stepped in front of him. 'Before you go, perhaps you'd like to return Jessica's key,' he said pleasantly.

'For a new friend, you're taking a lot upon yourself.'

Gregory fiddled bad-temperedly with his key ring and finally extracted the door-key.

'I shan't say it was a pleasure to meet you,' he snarled, and went out slamming the door behind him.

There was silence for a minute then Jessica subsided into the nearest chair.

'I'm sorry,' she said in a low voice. 'What an embarrassing scene. I never dreamt he might be here.'

'Of course not,' Ian soothed. 'You look pale. Can I get you something? Tea, perhaps?'

'Tea would be lovely. The kitchen's through there.' Jessica leaned back in the chair and closed her eyes.

Ian was soon back with a tray of tea which he placed on a little table.

'I hope these are the right cups.' He picked up the teapot. 'Not precious family heirlooms?'

'My grandmother left them to me,' she said tonelessly. 'But I like to use them.'

Again there was silence, then Ian said, 'So that was Gregory. He's quite good-looking,' he admitted. 'At least, he would be if he wasn't in such a bad temper.'

'He's brought everything upon himself,' she said wearily. 'It was his choice to break the engagement, not mine.'

'And how do you feel about it now?' He looked at her intently.

'I think I had a lucky escape.'

'No regrets?'

She shook her head. 'I wish I'd never got engaged. In fact, I wish I'd never met him. I hate the position we're in now

— rows, explanations, disappointment for my mother and his. But no, I have no regrets that I'm not going to marry him.'

'You're too good for him,' Ian said firmly. 'But you still have to tell your parents. Until you do, you can't really be said to be free.'

'I suppose not. I'm not looking forward to that.' She looked down at her fingers, twisting in her lap.

'So what are your plans for the future?' he asked, trying to sound bright.

They're obviously not to include you, she thought bitterly. Perhaps it would have been better if she'd never met him either. She forced herself to smile.

'Not to bother about boyfriends. From now on, I'll concentrate on my business. I want to make a real success of it.'

'You will,' he said. 'I know it.' He took the tray into the kitchen and she could hear him washing up. He was soon back.

'I'll go and get your cases and bags,' he said.

Jessica watched him from the window.

He looked up at her and waved, and for a moment she was back in Italy where the sun often caught the blond lights in his hair. She bit her lip. Yes, Gregory was quite good-looking, but Ian was more than that. He was special.

He appeared in the bedroom door-way with two cases. 'D'you want these in here?'

'Yes, please, and the art stuff in the studio.' She led the way to a small room where she kept her painting equipment. An easel stood beside a battered table in the centre of the room. Canvases were piled against the walls and shelves were crowded with all the paraphernalia of the artist. Ian looked around with interest.

'It has a large window,' Jessica said, 'so the light's not too bad.'

He looked at his watch. 'I'd better phone for a taxi. There's a train back in half an hour.'

By the time the taxi arrived, they had run out of casual remarks. Jessica was almost glad to hear the ring at her bell. She'd already thanked him for his help and for driving her home. He put his hands on her shoulders in his usual gesture and kissed her on the forehead.

'Could we make a date for next week?' he suggested.

'I don't know where I'll be,' she said evasively. 'I'll probably spend some time with my parents and then . . . well, I don't know.'

He gave her an enigmatic look as if seeing something behind the hesitant words. 'We'll be in touch,' he said. 'Goodbye, Jessica.'

Then he was gone. She wanted to rush to her bedroom window and watch the taxi until it disappeared, but she forced herself to resist. She didn't want him to look up and find her watching him again.

'Goodbye, my darling,' she whispered and tears ran unchecked down her cheeks.

For a few minutes she allowed them to fall before reaching for a tissue. What a silly way to behave, she berated herself, crying over a man who didn't want her. The second man who didn't want her, she corrected herself. Well, she didn't need any man. She had her career and intended to be the best she could. She blew her nose. Hilly had invited her to stay at the villa in the autumn. She would look forward to that.

Beginning to make plans, she went into the bedroom and changed into jeans and a jumper. Then she picked up the telephone. There was one man who would always want her. He answered at once.

'Hello, poppet, lovely to hear you. Where are you?'

'I'm in my flat. Dad, can I come and stay for a few days? But I've hurt my ankle so I can't drive.'

'Give me half an hour,' said her father, 'and I'll be over to get you.'

Thoughtfully Jessica replaced the phone. There would be no way to avoid a showdown with her mother if she was staying with them, but it would be a relief to get everything out into the open.

She hobbled into the bedroom to pack some clean clothes, musing that that was all she seemed to do these days.

* * *

Ian sat in the train speeding towards Breverton, gazing out of the window but seeing nothing of the landscape flashing past. Instead, he was seeing again Jessica's face as she'd reacted to his suggestion of a date next week. He'd expected a smile, a look of pleasure, but she had been evasive, awkward even. Clearly she'd found the idea unwelcome. Why?

They'd had a lovely time in Italy; become really close friends. It had been difficult not to carry feelings of friendship beyond the boundaries he'd set. What would she have done if he'd really set out to make her fall for him? But that wouldn't have been fair. They'd both agreed the rules before they went. She'd made it clear she wanted nothing but friendship from him. And to start with, that was what he'd wanted from her. At first.

But then she'd begun to get under his skin. He, the cool Ian Grantly, the man for whom girls fell at the first smile, was uncertain what to do. For the first time in his adult life, he'd found a girl who was impervious to his charms, who cared less for him than he did for her.

Was the reason that idiot Gregory? Did she really still love him and intend to get him back?

She denied it, said she'd had a lucky escape. But what did Shakespeare say? Methinks the lady doth protest too much. Was she just trying to convince herself?

He wished Hilly was staying in England for a while longer, then he could have discussed it with her. But she was leaving for Lake Garda tomorrow. Should he phone her when she arrived in Italy? No, it wasn't the sort of thing you could discuss on the telephone. He put his head back and closed his eyes. What should he do?

Home

'Isn't this nice!' Jessica's mother looked round the dining table with satisfaction. 'Just like it used to be.'

'It's lovely to have some of your home cooking again,' said Jessica, knowing the remark would please her mother. 'Nobody makes steak pie like you.'

She'd been home for three days and no one had mentioned Gregory. She knew how difficult it was for her mother to keep silent on the subject and suspected that her father had warned her to say nothing until Jessica did.

I'll have to say something soon, Jessica thought as she cut into the crisp pastry and released the delicious aroma of steak and kidney.

But once she did, there would be no going back and an avalanche of questions and reproaches would descend on her. I'll wait a while, she decided.

When the meal was over, she settled down to manicure her nails. Her father went into the garden to water his flower beds and her mother sat on the couch next to Jessica with some coloured squares of material.

'What are you doing now?' asked Jessica. 'Making a patchwork quilt?'

'That's right,' replied her mother placidly. 'Susan and I are trying a new craft. She's better at it than me, but she's been doing it for longer.'

'It'll be very pretty,' Jessica commented, fingering the slippery satin and textured brocade. 'You have some lovely material.'

'You can buy packs of a dozen different squares. They're pretty, aren't they?'

Jessica returned to her nails.

'When is your friend returning to Italy?' her mother asked a few minutes later. They chatted companionably about Hilly for a while then fell silent again.

Jessica looked around the neat sitting-room, enjoying the peace. They'd decided not to watch television until the news later on. A clock ticked gently on the mantelpiece. The scent of fresh flowers mingled with the wax polish her mother used so assiduously.

I did right to come home for a few days, Jessica thought. Already she felt calmer and ready to start painting again soon. Her ankle was much better, too, after the rest because her parents refused to let her do anything other than sit with her foot on a stool.

Suddenly her mother dropped her work into her lap.

'I'm sorry, I just can't not say anything, whatever your father says. Have you and Gregory had a row? I don't understand why you're not seeing each other. You've been here three days and he hasn't called or even phoned.'

'Actually, I have seen him,' said Jessica quietly. 'He was at the flat when I got back from Hilly's.'

Her mother smiled. 'That's all right then. I thought you hadn't seen him since you went away. So is he coming round?' Mrs Lawrence picked up her handiwork again. 'You must have a lot to talk about.'

Jessica's father came into the room and, sensing the direction the conversation had taken, gave his wife a warning glance which she chose to ignore.

'Come on, Jessica, let's see if you can beat me at backgammon yet,' he said, going to a cupboard and lifting out the game. 'You never could when you lived at home.'

Thankfully Jessica got to her feet. Saved from explanations again! But it couldn't go on for ever. She would have to come clean soon.

★ ★ ★

'So what have you decided to call her?' Jessica cradled the tiny baby in her arms, marvelling at the perfection of the little snub nose and rosebud mouth.

'Delyth,' said Kay. 'It's Welsh. It means beautiful girl.'

'Oh, I like that. Delyth,' Jessica repeated. 'It's very sweet. It suits her.' She smiled at her friend. She and Kay had been friends since childhood. 'Shall we take her to the park? Show her off?'

They sat on a seat in the park by a wide sparkling lake. Ducks paddled and bobbed busily then made their way to the water's edge hoping for bread to be thrown. Delyth was asleep.

'I'll bring her here to feed the ducks when she's older,' said Kay.

'Kay,' Jessica said at length, 'would you do me a favour? If you're not busy, would you come to my flat on Saturday morning? Gregory's coming to collect some books and CDs and I — I don't want to be alone with him.'

Kay looked at her curiously. 'Don't want to be alone with your fiancé?'

Jessica sighed. 'Actually Gregory is no longer my fiancé.'

'I wondered why you weren't wearing your ring. I didn't like to ask.'

Jessica told her how Gregory's feelings had changed. 'But I haven't told my parents yet. I'm waiting for the right moment.'

'I'm so sorry,' said Kay. 'What time shall I come?'

* * *

'This is just a thought,' said Mrs Lawrence, as they sat with their coffee after dinner, 'but would it be a good idea for both families to get together one evening soon?'

Jessica didn't need to ask which two families.

'Susan and I are concerned that something's not right between you and Gregory. If either of you is worried about something we could thrash out the problem between us. You know we only have your best interests at heart.'

Jessica took a steadying breath. The time had come . . .

'You'd better know — Gregory and I aren't getting married.'

'What?' Her mother's expression was one of disbelief. 'Susan doesn't know this. Gregory hasn't said anything to her. What made you take such a dreadful decision? Everything was fine between you two until you went to Hilly's house and off to Italy. Have you met someone else? That's it, isn't it? You've thrown Gregory over for another man. How could you?'

Jessica felt herself flush guiltily. A vision of Ian's face floated before her eyes. If only she could say, 'Yes, and he's everything Gregory isn't.'

'What about your dress and the invitations? Aunt Jenny is planning to come all the way from Australia. Oh, dear!' Mrs Lawrence's eyes filled with tears. 'How could you, Jessica?'

The girl gazed helplessly at her mother, feeling a strong sense of guilt even though the decision to end the engagement had not been hers.

'Mum, please.' She patted her mother's hand. 'It was Gregory's decision, not mine.'

'I don't believe you.' The woman snatched her hand away. 'He loves you. You're just putting the blame on him.'

Jessica's father came in hurriedly from his study. 'What's going on? I heard raised voices . . . '

'Oh, Jeff,' his wife wailed, 'Jessica has

just told me she doesn't want to marry Gregory.'

'No,' Jessica protested, 'it wasn't my decision. Gregory changed his mind.'

Her father sighed and sat down next to his tearful wife, gesturing to Jessica to leave it to him . . .

★   ★   ★

On Saturday morning, Jessica drove to her flat. She'd been there only ten minutes when Kay arrived with Delyth in her pram.

'I'll feel terribly in the way,' she protested.

'You won't have to say anything. I just don't want to be alone with him. I don't want to talk to him and he'll go all the sooner if there's someone here.'

'What shall you do now if you're not going to get married?' Kay asked.

'Carry on with my painting,' said Jessica. 'I've quite a few commissions lined up. I'll be very busy.'

'No other man in view?'

Jessica longed to talk about Ian, to tell Kay of the wonderful time they'd had in Italy, but she'd have to finish by saying that Ian didn't want her, and that would be too embarrassing.

'No,' she answered, firmly and untruthfully. 'No other man.'

There was a ring at the doorbell. Jessica had put Gregory's books and CDs in a box in the little entrance hall, hoping to give them to him at the door. But he pushed past her and into the sitting-room. He didn't notice Kay curled up in an armchair in the corner.

'Jessica, I think we should talk,' he began.

'You remember Kay, don't you?' she said quickly. 'She's brought her baby to show me.'

Kay gave him a nervous smile.

He turned back to Jessica. 'Very clever,' he said, 'but you can't hide for ever. There are things we need to discuss.'

'I suppose there are,' said Jessica wearily, 'but let's leave them for another time.'

'Did you tell your parents about that man — what was his name — Grantly?' Gregory asked in a spiteful tone.

'There's nothing to tell. He's just a friend who was helping out.'

'I don't believe you.'

'It doesn't matter what you believe,' Jessica returned with spirit. 'You chose to end the engagement. What I do now or who I see is no concern of yours.' She picked up the box and opened the front door. 'I think you'll find everything is here.'

With a furious glare he took the box and marched out.

Jessica returned to the sitting-room and collapsed into an armchair.

Kay looked at her curiously. 'Grantly?'

'Ian Grantly. A friend,' said Jessica. 'He brought me back from Hilly's house when I hurt my ankle and couldn't drive.'

'Gregory seems to think he's more than a friend.'

'What does he know? He only met him for a moment. He was here when we arrived and got the wrong idea.'

'For a man who ended the engagement himself, he's very concerned with your affairs.'

'Tell me about it,' said Jessica bitterly. 'I wish he'd go and find someone else.'

'So this Ian is no-one special? Just a friend?'

She was startled to see tears spring into Jessica's eyes and spill over.

'Jessica! What is it?' She went to her friend, holding her hand.

Jessica couldn't speak. The floodgates were open. The emotion she had been keeping in check was finally released.

'It's this Ian, isn't it? He *is* someone special.'

Jessica reached for a tissue and rubbed at her eyes.

'I'm sorry,' she said. 'It's just that I haven't been able to talk about him, and I think I *need* to talk.'

Kay nodded and waited. That was the good thing about her, Jessica thought, she had endless patience.

'Ian is Hilly's cousin,' Jessica began. 'We met at a party when I was painting

Hilly's house.' Looking down at her hands, twisting her fingers together, she told Kay all about Ian.

'I went on holiday to Italy,' she said, 'with Hilly and her mother. Ian joined us for a few days. We were able to spend some time together. It was wonderful.'

'I don't understand,' said Kay. 'What was wrong with that?'

'I fell in love with him.' Jessica's voice was quiet. She paused, then went on, 'But we'd agreed before we went that there were to be no emotional complications. Ian doesn't want a serious relationship and I'd just had that shock announcement from Gregory, so we weren't looking for anything but friendship. We were just companions.'

'But things changed?'

'For me — yes. The surroundings didn't help: sun, romantic scenery, music, warm scented evenings. It might have been better if he'd kept me at arm's length, but he's not like that.'

'But you don't think he fell for you?'

Jessica shook her head. 'I think he

believes I'll go back to Gregory. He feels nothing for me but friendship. But that's not enough for me. So I must never see him again.' The tears began anew and she scrubbed furiously at her eyes. 'Phew — now that I've told you, can I ask you to keep it to yourself? Neither Gregory nor my parents must know.'

* * *

Jessica returned to her parents' house in the late afternoon. Her mother was in the kitchen, cooking. She turned a furious face to Jessica as the girl opened the door.

'Ian Grantly!' Mrs Lawrence banged a saucepan of potatoes on to the work surface. 'You said there was no one else. So who's this Ian Grantly?'

'How do you — ?' Jessica began.

'Gregory's been here, very upset. He's met this man, he says, so you can't deny his existence.' She added a lump of butter and thumped the potatoes with a masher. 'So that's why you threw poor Gregory over.'

'I didn't throw him over. Didn't he also tell you that it was his idea to call off the wedding? He's frightened of marriage. He probably doesn't want to leave his mother,' she added bitterly.

'You could persuade him. Make him see sense.'

'I'm not going to persuade any man to marry me against his will!'

'But the preparations! What are we going to do about the dress and the cake?'

'I'm sure they'll take the dress back, and I don't suppose they've made the cake yet. I'll do some phoning round tomorrow. Don't worry about it, Mum.'

'But Susan . . . '

'I think it's Susan you're more worried about!' she raged. 'Well, I'm not afraid of her. She'll have to understand that her precious son doesn't want to get married.'

Half an hour later, she had packed her suitcase.

'You're not going?' Her mother put out a hand to stop her. 'I've just made dinner.'

'I'm not hungry, thank you. I'll make a sandwich later. I'll be over later for the rest of my clothes. Thanks for having me. But now I must get on with my painting.' She gave a bitter laugh. 'If I'm not to be married, I must become a successful businesswoman.'

'What about this other man? Aren't you going to marry him?'

'Gregory doesn't want me, and Ian doesn't want me either,' she said, her voice bitter and lost.

'That's That'

'Well, that's that,' said Jessica as she closed the door of her flat behind her. 'That's put it into words. Gregory doesn't want me and Ian doesn't want me.'

But I shan't cry, she told herself, there's nothing worse than self pity.

She went into her little studio and began to sort her paintings, placing the half-finished canvas of the Cornish cottage on the easel ready for the morning. She considered. Quite good, Caro would be pleased.

When the doorbell rang Gregory was the last person she expected.

'May I come in?' he said, looking smug.

'Have we anything left to say to each other?' she asked with a sigh.

'I think so. Are you on your own? Every time I've seen you lately, you've had someone here. We've hardly talked on our own.'

'But you made your position clear and I've accepted it. There's no more to say.' She made to close the door but he put his hand against it.

'Let me come in, just for ten minutes. I think you might be pleased at what I have to say when you've thought about it.'

They stood facing each other in the centre of the sitting-room. Jessica didn't invite him to sit down.

'I've got something of yours,' Gregory began.

She looked at him suspiciously. He lifted her left hand and before she could stop him, had slipped the engagement ring back on her finger. She looked at it in disbelief.

'I still love you, Jessica. I think we should start over,' he said. 'I'm prepared to overlook your friendship with — what was his name — Ian Grantly. That episode wasn't really your fault. We won't mention it again.'

She was almost speechless. 'You're prepared to — what?'

'Let me finish.' He held up an imperious hand. 'Your mother told me that Grantly has rejected you. I must say that doesn't show him in a very good light. But I would hate you to have to bear two disappointments. And I do still love you. I've thought things over and discussed it with our mothers and I'm prepared to go ahead with the wedding. And we won't mention any of this again.'

Jessica tore the ring from her hand and threw it at him.

'You're prepared to go ahead, are you?' she raged. 'Well, let me tell you, too much has happened to start over. I don't love you, and I don't believe you love me. What basis is that for marriage?'

Gregory retrieved the ring and stood holding it uncertainly.

'I can function perfectly well without a man — any man,' Jessica went on. 'I have my painting and I intend to concentrate on that.'

'But, Jessica ... ' He held out a placating hand.

'Please go. And don't ever come back.' She moved to the window and stood looking out with unseeing eyes. How dare he think that she would take him back or, rather, be prepared to be taken back by him?

'Well, if that's the way you feel — ' His tone was a mixture of hurt and outrage. Clearly he felt he had offered her a great deal.

The ring at the doorbell startled them both. Jessica didn't move. With a glance at her, Gregory moved to open the door himself.

Ian stepped into the room. Seeming not to notice Gregory, he crossed the room to Jessica. 'Sorry to call so late, but I've been in Birmingham all day. I had to make sure you were all right. I rang your mother's house and she said you were here. She didn't sound very pleased.'

'She's not,' said Jessica in a tight voice.

'How's the ankle?'

The door slammed and they both turned quickly. Gregory, his face red with fury, glared at Ian from across the room.

'What are you doing here?' he demanded. 'Leave my fiancée alone. You don't want her and I do. She won't see sense until you leave her alone.'

As Ian looked at her in surprise, Jessica took a step towards Gregory.

'No, *you* go,' she said. 'I'm not your fiancée and I never will be again.'

'Look — this is obviously a bad time,' said Ian. 'I'll go. We can speak later. I only came to make sure you're all right.'

'Yes, go!' Gregory was almost dancing with rage. 'You keep turning up when you're not wanted. Jessica and I were discussing . . . '

Jessica marched to the door and flung it open. 'Out!' she ordered. 'Now. And don't ever come back. Whatever our mothers say.'

He slunk off, and she threw herself

into an armchair, saying nothing. Ian took the chair opposite, equally silent.

'I'm sorry,' Jessica said at last, giving him a weak smile. 'I always seem to be apologising to you for Gregory's scenes.'

'Why did he come?'

She gave a deep, shuddering sigh. 'To tell me he's prepared to overlook my behaviour and go ahead with the wedding.'

She still could hardly believe it.

'And you said?' Ian asked at last.

'I think you can imagine! He had discussed it with our mothers . . . Can you believe it? What did I ever see in him?'

'So you've finished with him, finally and irrevocably?'

'I have.' They looked at each other, and Jessica, whose emotions were already at fever pitch, began to feel the tingling sensation she'd felt when they danced in Italy. Ian could be in no doubt now that she was free. But he said nothing and she felt mortified. So he really didn't want her. He'd meant it when he'd said they'd just be friends.

She jumped to her feet.

'Would you like a glass of wine before you go? I've got a rather nice Spanish one.' She darted into the kitchen.

Men! Were any of them worth a second's attention? She was about to return with the wine when Ian's mobile phone rang.

'Donna!' she heard him say. Then he was quiet listening to the person at the other end until she heard an explosion of laughter and, 'Donna, you're wonderful! I love you. I'll see you tomorrow, early.'

As she entered the room, he was replacing the phone in his pocket, a wide smile on his face. He realised Jessica had heard him and patted his pocket.

'Good news,' he said. 'I must be getting back now. I'll call again tomorrow if I may. Will the wine keep till then?'

'I'm going out tomorrow. I'll ring you.' She went with him to the door.

'You won't forget? Promise?' He

looked at her anxiously. 'We must meet soon. There's lots to talk about.' He gave her a quick kiss on each cheek and was gone.

She didn't watch him from her window but returned to her armchair. His words rang in her ears: 'Donna, you're wonderful. I love you.'

It hadn't taken him long to find someone else. Why did he want to see her again, she wondered resentfully. And what could they have to discuss? Her mind was in a whirl. First Gregory, then Ian. Why should she bother about either of these men?

* * *

Two days later, Hilly phoned Jessica. 'Has something happened? Ian seems a bit put out that you haven't phoned him.'

'I promised I'd ring and I will.'

'I think he's concerned because every time he visits your flat, your fiancé is there.'

'Ex-fiancé. He keeps turning up uninvited.'

'Ian seems to think you might go back to him.'

'For goodness sake, what must I do to convince him? I'm so tired of men and their refusal to listen.'

Hilly was sympathetic. 'You really are having problems, aren't you? I'll try to convince Ian and I'll tell him you'll phone soon, shall I?'

Jessica hesitated, then, 'Yes, do that, please, Hilly. We had such a lovely time in Italy. We must remain friends at least.'

'Ian's a good catch, you know,' Hilly said. 'He has his own company and it's doing very well.'

'He had business meetings in Italy,' said Jessica. 'He didn't take many photographs though he told me he was a photo-journalist. What exactly does he do?'

'He's the managing director of a greetings card company,' Hilly told her. 'I don't know why he told you he's a

271

photo-journalist. Perhaps it sounded more glamorous.'

'Greetings cards,' Jessica echoed thoughtfully. 'What's the name of the company?'

When Hilly told her, it was the name of the company that had rejected her. She'd told Ian about the interview. He'd said nothing about owning the company, but then he couldn't if he wanted them to be friends. She might have refused to have anything more to do with him. Hence the story about being a photo-journalist. A thought struck her.

'I had an interview with them some time ago. The man who interviewed me said he was the director. But his name wasn't Grantly.'

'That'd have been Ian's stepfather. He died a year ago.' There was a little pause then Hilly said, 'Jessica, I may be speaking out of turn, but I think Ian's very much in love with you.'

'You're wrong, and I can prove it. When he was in my flat, he got a phone call.' Her voice trembled. 'From someone called Donna. He said he loved her.'

Hilly began to laugh. 'Did you ask him about Donna?'

'Of course not. It was a private call. But it proves he doesn't love me.'

'Oh, Jessica.' Hilly was still laughing. 'Donna is forty, happily married and has two lovely little boys. She's Ian's secretary,' she finished. 'So whatever the reason for what you heard, it certainly didn't mean he loves her.'

Time For Honesty

Jessica made an early start on her painting the next morning. To her amazement, she'd slept well. Now she entered her little studio ready to put out of her mind all thoughts except those of her painting.

Most of the background was done and the walls and roof of the cottage. What remained was her favourite task, the finer details.

There was an old wooden bench near the front door, surrounded by tubs of scarlet geraniums and piles of large shells. Jessica mixed the colours and selected a brush.

The doorbell rang. She hesitated, longing to ignore it. But with a sigh, she replaced the brush and went to the door.

'My little mother hen has ordered me to visit you,' Ian announced. 'She said she spoke to you last night on the phone.'

He looked at her speculatively. 'You didn't phone and you don't look pleased to see me.' He glanced around. 'All alone?'

'Yes. I'm painting.'

'Ah. So you don't want to be disturbed.' There was a pause. 'But I'm afraid I can't go. There's something I want to discuss with you.'

'Won't it wait?'

'Not for a moment. It's life and death. We could discuss it over lunch,' he said hopefully.

'But it's not lunchtime.'

'It will be once you've changed and removed the green paint from the end of your nose.'

'We could have something here,' she suggested, 'then I needn't change.'

'Lazy girl. Go and make yourself beautiful. Correction, even more beautiful. I don't want to eat here, it has unpleasant memories!'

She looked up quickly, but he was smiling sweetly at her.

The Fox and Goose was built on the edge of the canal with a pretty flower-filled terrace overlooking the water.

'Outside or in?' he asked.

'Let's eat out here.' Jessica indicated a table near the waterside. 'It's hardly Lake Garda but there are quite a few boats to watch.'

Ian handed her a menu. 'I'll give the order and get some drinks. Don't go away.'

She watched him thread his way through the tables and disappear into the bar. What are you doing here? she admonished herself.

She looked out over the water, seeing not the grey wash of an English canal but the blue-green expanse of an Italian lake. They'd had such a lovely time, the day they crossed to the island, just the two of them, with no thought of the life that awaited them at home.

Lost in a reverie, she didn't notice Ian's return until he placed two glasses on the table and sat down. 'Penny for your thoughts.'

Jessica started. 'I was remembering the lake.'

He put a hand over hers. 'We had a wonderful time, didn't we? I can't wait to go back.'

'You're going back?'

'Of course. And so are you.'

'To start on my commissions — yes. That has to be arranged.' She toyed with the glass, a thoughtful look on her face. 'I spoke to Hilly,' she said at last. 'She told me about your company.'

He guessed what she meant. 'Ah,' he said. 'But when you came for an interview, my stepfather was the managing director.'

'Do you know why they gave the position to someone else?'

'It was a fix,' he admitted. 'The job had been promised to the nephew of his best customer.'

'Thank you for being honest.'

Their meal arrived and occupied their attention for a while.

At last Jessica sat back with a sigh. 'That was lovely. Thank you. I hadn't realised how hungry I was.'

She was longing to know what they had to discuss, but was determined not to ask.

'Do you remember the night we met?' he asked. 'I thought you were the loveliest girl at the party.'

She gave him a shy smile. 'And the most difficult.'

'That too,' he agreed. 'But you intrigued me. You didn't fall into my arms. You were different. You were a challenge.' He rested his chin on his hand. 'What did you think of me at first?'

She gave him a straight look. 'You were an aggravation.'

He sat back in his chair. 'And now?'

'I don't think that any longer,' she admitted.

'Do you think we get on well?'

'Of course,' she said.

'Well enough to spend the rest of our lives together?'

Her eyes widened. 'Is this a proposal?'

'Yes. Unless you'd like me to get

down on one knee. So what's your answer?'

'I don't think I heard a proposal. Not a proper one. Anyway, there's a problem.'

He sat upright. 'What do you mean?'

Jessica looked down at her fingers twisting together on the table.

Ian took her hand in his. 'Darling Jessica, I love you. Will you marry me?'

She hesitated. 'What about the . . . problem?'

He sighed. 'Tell me.'

'You said you don't want to lose your freedom. How do I know you really want to get married? Perhaps you'll change your mind.'

'We'll be married tomorrow, if you like, then I can't change my mind. Not that I'd ever want to. I don't want my freedom. I want to be tied to you for ever. I love you more than anything in the world. Now will you put me out of my misery? Darling Jessica, will you marry me?'

Their heads were close together. She

turned her face and their lips met.

'Yes, Ian,' she said softly, 'I will.'

He looked into her eyes. 'We can't stay here,' he said. 'That's not a proper kiss for a newly-engaged couple. Come on.' He took her hand and led her down the steps to the tow path.

Arms around each other, they strolled along the edge of the water until they reached the overhanging branches of a willow tree where Ian took her in his arms.

'Now I can really show you how much I love you,' he said huskily.

After just one long, lingering kiss, Jessica was convinced. But he gave her several more, just to be sure.

THE END

We do hope that you have enjoyed reading this large print book.

Did you know that all of our titles are available for purchase?

We publish a wide range of high quality large print books including:
Romances, Mysteries, Classics
General Fiction
Non Fiction and Westerns

Special interest titles available in large print are:
The Little Oxford Dictionary
Music Book, Song Book
Hymn Book, Service Book

Also available from us courtesy of Oxford University Press:
Young Readers' Dictionary
(large print edition)
Young Readers' Thesaurus
(large print edition)

For further information or a free brochure, please contact us at:
Ulverscroft Large Print Books Ltd.,
The Green, Bradgate Road, Anstey,
Leicester, LE7 7FU, England.
Tel: (00 44) **0116 236 4325**
Fax: (00 44) **0116 234 0205**

WOMBAT CREEK

Noelene Jenkinson

Single mother Summer Dalton arrives from New South Wales to her grandfather's small farm in the Western District. However, memories of her hippy parents' banishment for their free-loving morals — decades before — remain. Her hope is to settle on the land she's inherited, so she refuses her new neighbour Ethan Bourke's offer to buy her out. Then, a jealous old flame and Ethan's disapproving mother come into the mix. Can Summer and Ethan resolve their growing attraction to one another?

ACKNOWLEDGEMENTS

With special thanks to my wonderful editor and mentor, Claire Bord and all the amazing people at Bookouture who have helped bring this book to life and to the inimitable Kim Nash. Thanks to my fabulous agent, Madeleine Milburn and to Hayley Steed and all at the MM agency, my inspirational friend Kelly (and the girls) and to my beautiful sister and mummy – my life support – and my boys, Louie and Felix. And to my best boy ever, David. The summer of 2018 changed my life forever. I will never forget it. The gods put us together and I love you more than all the words I could ever write in a lifetime.

CPSIA information can be obtained
at www.ICGtesting.com
Printed in the USA
LVHW091708260419
615695LV00013B/486/P